The Home School Detectives

THE MYSTERY AT THE
BROKEN BRIDGE

John Bibee

InterVarsity Press
Downers Grove, Illinois

© 1997 by John Bibee

InterVarsity Press® is the book-publishing division of InterVarsity Christian Fellowship®, a student movement active on campus at hundreds of universities, colleges and schools of nursing in the United States of America, and a member movement of the International Fellowship of Evangelical Students. For information about local and regional activities, write Public Relations Dept., InterVarsity Christian Fellowship, 6400 Schroeder Rd., P.O. Box 7895, Madison, WI 53707-7895.

Cover illustration: David Darrow

ISBN 0-8308-1916-9

Printed in the United States of America ∞

Library of Congress Cataloging in Publication Data

Bibee, John.
   The mystery at the broken bridge / John Bibee.
      p.   cm.—(The Home School Detectives ; 6)
   Summary: The Home School Detectives are glad to help members of the Springdale Community Church fix up a run-down apartment project, until Josh's new basketball disappears and Josh is suspected of taking a woman's purse.
   ISBN 0-8308-1916-9 (alk. paper)
   [1. Christian life—Fiction.   2. Stealing—Fiction.   3. Inner cities—Fiction.   4. Mystery and detective stories.]   I. Title.
II. Series: Bibee, John.   Home School Detectives ; 6.
PZ7.B471464Mr   1997
   [Fic]—dc21
                                              96-37894
                                                  CIP
                                                      AC

16	15	14	13	12	11	10	9	8	7	6	5	4	3	2	1
10	09	08	07	06	05	04	03	02	01	00	99	98	97		

1. Basketball Steal _____ 5

2. Police Report _____ 17

3. Josh Accused _____ 30

4. Under the Broken Bridge_____ 41

5. The Bridgewood Thief_____ 52

6. A Good Friday? _____ 65

7. The Meeting at Eight _____ 77

8. Drew Road_____ 89

9. What the Boys Saw _____ 99

10. The Setup_____ 105

11. The Bridge Across the Gulf _____ 116

Chapter One

Basketball Steal

The Good Friday picnic at the Bridgewood Apartments was going well until Josh Morgan discovered that his brand-new basketball was missing.

"I can't believe it's missing," Josh fumed. "I worked three months for that ball. I mowed lawns, washed floors, and took care of Mrs. Wimple's nasty cat, Fiffi. It was the best ball I ever had."

"I know, Josh," Carlos said. "You've only told us a hundred times."

"It had a real leather cover too," Josh mumbled.

"We know that too," Billy added, rolling his eyes. "It was official size and weight, just like the NBA . . ."

Josh had brought it to the work day/cookout so that he and the other kids could play at the new backboard and goal that had been set up that morning.

"The church donated some basketballs," Billy said.

"Yeah, three of them," Carlos said. "They're not expensive, but they work okay."

"I know, but I wanted to play with my new ball," Josh said. "You know how it is."

"So did someone else," Billy said.

"I can't believe those guys took it," Josh said angrily after he finished eating the last bit of his hamburger. He glared at the group of kids hanging out under the broken bridge near the Bridgewood Apartments. He knew some of their names. The kids under the bridge were eating hamburgers and hot dogs, laughing and joking with one another.

"They act like nothing even happened," Carlos Brown said.

"Yeah," Billy Renner agreed. "We're out here trying to do something nice and these guys steal from us."

"You don't know for a fact that they took it," Julie Brown said softly.

"Of course they took it," Josh said bitterly. "It didn't just dribble off by itself. Carlos and Billy and I looked everywhere: down in the creek bed, in the hedges."

"Did you look under the broken bridge?" Julie asked.

"I especially looked around under there," Josh said. "It's just gone."

"Yeah," Carlos agreed. "It's gone. Long gone."

"And they said that none of them took it or saw anything," Billy said. "It makes me really mad. I think we should go interrogate each one and see who is lying."

Billy Renner jumped up off the picnic bench to start the investigation.

"Hold on." Rebecca Renner pulled her twin brother back down to his place on the picnic bench. The others nodded in approval. Billy Renner was always quick on the trigger—sometimes too quick.

"But we're the Home School Detectives," Billy said. "People expect us to solve mysteries. If we keep asking questions, one of them is bound to feel guilty and spill his guts."

"Hang on, Sherlock." Rebecca grabbed her brother by the back of his shirt again. Billy sat down, a frown on his face. "You haven't even finished eating."

The five other kids at the picnic table nodded. They all knew about Billy's impulsive side because all of them had raced to keep up with it at one time or another. In two seconds he had forgotten that just a minute before he was talking about how hungry he was and that he could eat three hamburgers. He had settled for two burgers, a huge stack of potato chips and two cans of soda. But he was ready to forget his hunger as soon as he started thinking about how to get the basketball back. The others had already finished their food, but Billy had been talking while the others were eating.

The six of them, Josh and Emily Morgan, Billy and Rebecca Renner, and Julie and Carlos Brown, had been known as the Home School Detectives around Springdale ever since they had helped the police solve a thirty-year-old mystery. Since that time, they had solved a number of mysteries and gained a reputation for being effective detectives.

"What did your dad say about your basketball?" Julie asked sympathetically.

"He said that maybe it will turn up," Josh said in disgust.

"Well, maybe it will." Emily felt sorry for her brother. She and Josh shot baskets at home. Now they would have to use the old basketball, which was already worn out and smooth from so much use.

"I know someone stole it," Josh said angrily. "I never should have let those bridge kids use it."

"Yeah, I bet they know what really happened," Billy said. "They're just lying to protect each other."

"But they might not have taken it," Julie insisted softly. "You guys really shouldn't accuse people without knowing the facts."

"What do you mean?" Josh demanded. "I let them use it while we were working inside, cleaning out the rec room. They stole it and you know it."

"But Ricky Carson said he set it down by the barbecue grill when they lined up to get hamburgers," Julie said.

"That's what he claims," Josh said with contempt. "He could be lying to protect himself if he's the thief."

"But what if he is telling the truth?" Julie asked.

"Ricky said that when they got up near the grill to get their food, they noticed that the basketball was gone," Rebecca added. "Someone could have taken it, but it could have been anyone. It might have been someone from our church and not the kids here."

"None of our church friends would steal my basketball," Josh said. "Do you really believe that?"

"I don't," Billy said. "How can you accuse people in your own church of doing something like that without any facts?"

"Well, Josh is accusing the Bridgewood kids without any facts," Julie said.

"But they had the basketball last," Josh almost yelled. "That is a fact, and in my mind that makes them the prime suspects."

He propped his elbows on the picnic table and looked at the Bridgewood Apartment kids with disgust. Everyone else seemed to be having a good time.

"All I'm saying is that it's not fair to accuse *all* the Bridgewood kids of taking your ball," Julie said. "Maybe one of them took it, but it sounds like you're accusing all of them, and you can't lump people together like that."

"Well, Josh could be right," Billy said. "Some people say there are gangs over here on this side of town. If they're a gang, they'd stick up for each other and lie for each other. So they would be in it together."

"Yeah, they could be in gangs and be lying," Josh said.

"But you still don't know that for sure," Julie countered. She sighed. "It's too bad. Everything was going well. My dad is really excited about all the things getting done around here today. Mr. Gossett, the owner of the apartments, is really happy. At first my dad said Mr. Gossett was suspicious about us coming out here to help. But now that he knows us, he's really helping out. Opening up the storage room as a recreation room and buying the Ping-Pong table was really nice of him."

"The Ping-Pong table is great," Emily agreed. "It's brand-new."

Many people from the Springdale Community Church were working that Friday afternoon to make the apartments a nicer place to live. Some were carrying paint cans and paint brushes. Others had shovels and rakes. Some were still inside working on the apartments. The six children had been helping cut the grass and pull weeds and clean the new recreation room.

The Bridgewood Apartments were known all over Springdale as a place where lower-income people lived. There were several old people living in the apartments, as well as many single mothers and lots of children. Mary Kline, one of the young mothers living in the apartments, was a friend of Louise Jones, who was a member of the Springdale Community Church. When Mary's water heater broke and she was told she would have to wait a week to get it fixed, Mary told Louise her problem. Louise then asked some of the men in the church to help Mary.

The next day, two men and two boys from the church went to Mary's apartment and replaced her water heater. She was so excited and thankful that she told Mrs. Perkins and Mrs. May, two older women across the hallway. They needed help with their plugged-up sink and dripping faucet. After the men helped them, they realized there were lots of people in the apartments who could use help with one thing or another. Some of the older people, for instance, had lights that were out, but they were too frail to get up on ladders and change the bulbs.

The outside of the apartments was rundown and messy. There was a play area for the children, with a swing set and slide, but all of the swings were missing. The merry-go-round didn't turn and the steps to the slide were broken. At one time there had been a basketball hoop set up on a small cement court, but now there was only a bare pole; the backboard had been gone for years. The yard around the apartments was full of weeds and spots of bare dirt. Several walls had been spray painted with graffiti. The asphalt parking lot and sidewalks were also decorated with spray-painted messages and pictures.

Even the old bridge near the Bridgewood Apartments was falling down and dangerous to walk on. It was a large wooden footbridge that crossed a creek to a small park. Beyond the park was another apartment complex known as the Gateway

Apartments, which was also in poor shape, but not as bad as the Bridgewood Apartments.

The old broken bridge was a popular place even though it was falling apart. Lots of young people hung out below the bridge in the creek bed. Most of the kids who hung out there lived in the Bridgewood Apartments or the Gateway Apartments. Those kids had a bad reputation around town. Lots of people even referred to them as the "the bridge kids." Most assumed the graffiti sprayed on the walls of the Bridgewood Apartments came from them. Some people said they were members of gangs, though others said Springdale was too small to have gangs. There were lots of empty beer cans under the old bridge. Some said the bridge kids used drugs.

Several young people were down by the bridge talking and eating. They seemed to be having a good time. Josh looked at the group of kids with suspicion and disgust. Some were sitting on bicycles. Others were on foot. One girl was wearing in-line skates.

"I should have figured something like this would happen," Josh said. "Dad said I probably shouldn't bring my ball. But I did it anyway. I should have listened to him."

"You couldn't have known your ball would get stolen," Julie said.

"But I did know there is more crime in this part of town." Josh was still looking at the kids near the bridge.

"Why do you suppose that is?" Billy asked. "I mean, poorer people live here. It seems like there would be less to steal. You'd think thieves would go to the richer parts of town to steal things."

"They steal around our house too," Emily said. "I heard my mom talking with old Mrs. Harrington on the phone. She lives on the end of our street in that big old house. She said she was missing things out of her garage. I think she said a Weed-Eater is gone and something else."

"There is a regular crime wave in Springdale." Billy jumped with excitement. "I say it calls for us to break this case right now. Let's go!"

"Sit down!" the other kids said loudly.

"You guys are no fun." Billy sat down with an angry thump.

"I do want to ask a few more questions," Josh said to the others.

"What do you mean?" Emily saw that her brother was staring at the kids over by the bridge again. "Do you really think the bridge kids did it?"

"Well, I don't know about Mrs. Harrington's Weed-Eater, but I do think one of them stole my basketball," Josh said. "They have a reputation around town for causing lots of trouble."

"Let's go interrogate the suspects," Billy said.

"I think it's a mistake to go over there and accuse them," Julie said. "You want to start a fight?"

"I'm not going to start a fight," Josh replied. "But I'm not going to back down either. I want my ball back."

"We better go together," Carlos advised. "Those are tough kids. They get in fights a lot. I heard one of the moms telling my dad that she was afraid her son was getting involved in some kind of gang. She said he left home whenever he felt like it and would be gone for a long time."

"That doesn't mean he is in a gang," Emily said.

"Well, I'm just saying that this mom thought her son was in a gang," Carlos said.

"Who was it?" Billy asked curiously.

"I can't tell you," Carlos said. "My parents don't want us to talk about church stuff or things we overhear. They say that's gossip."

"Gossip?" Billy asked. "That's not gossip. That's just information. We're trying to find out who stole Josh's ball. We're detectives on a case."

"Carlos is right," Julie said. "Dad told us not to talk about stuff like that. He tries to keep private matters private, but sometimes we can't help overhearing things."

"Well, can we go over to the bridge and at least check things out?" Billy asked.

"All I want to do is ask a few more questions," Josh said and stood up.

"But I'm not finished eating!" Billy yelled out as his attention suddenly shifted back to his hunger.

"That's because you talk too much," Rebecca said flatly.

"We'll go dump our trash," Josh said to Billy. "We'll come back for you."

While Josh and the others picked up their paper plates, Billy hurriedly stuffed the remaining potato chips in his mouth. He chewed anxiously as he watched his friends walk away. He took a big gulp of orange soda, hoping to make the chips go down faster. He stuffed in the last bite of hamburger.

"I'm done!" Billy hopped up and followed his friends. After they dumped their paper plates and cups in a big green garbage bag, they walked across the newly cleaned basketball court. Josh looked up at the new backboard with its orange rim and bright white net.

"I only got to shoot one basket out here today," Josh said as they walked by the hoop.

"Maybe your basketball will turn up," Julie said. "Why don't we look around together before you go talk to those kids? You shouldn't go over there if you're mad."

"I have a right to be mad," Josh said. "My basketball is missing."

The kids under the broken bridge stopped talking as they saw Josh and his friends come down the creek bank. The old bridge was covered with bright spray-painted names and symbols. The largest picture of all was a large blue cross painted on a metal reinforcement plate on the side of the bridge. Underneath someone had spelled the name Jesus with the letter *S* written backwards.

"Hey, Ricky." Josh wasn't smiling.

"You find your ball yet?" Ricky Carson asked.

"No," Josh said glumly.

"I'm sure sorry about that," Ricky replied. "But I told you where I put it. None of us have seen it since then." The other kids nodded in agreement. Josh searched their faces.

"That ball cost me a lot of money," Josh said slowly. "I saved a long time to get it."

"I don't know what else to tell you," Ricky said.

"Those Gateway kids might have taken it," a tall boy named Chester Tucker said. "They're a bunch of thieves."

"Yeah, it could be them," Ricky agreed. "They like to come over here and cause trouble. They paint on our bridge."

"Yeah." Chester pointed to a black spray-painted scrawl above his head. "You see that? That's their Gateway letter *G* near the big blue cross."

Josh squinted at the picture. At first he didn't see it because the letter was so zigzagged and angular looking and ran on as one long line.

"It does look sort of like a *G* if you look at it in the right way," Julie said.

"Yeah, that's their sign," Ricky said. "They come over here and try to cause trouble. They do it all the time. But we run them off. We protect what's ours. This bridge is ours."

The other kids under the bridge nodded their heads and looked angry. Some of them were whispering.

"You guys were the last to have Josh's ball," Billy said suspiciously. "And I haven't seen any of the Gateway kids over here."

"Are you accusing me, Shorty?" Chester asked, stepping up to Billy and towering over him. He wore gray shorts, a dirty gray T-shirt and dirty white basketball shoes.

"We aren't accusing anyone, Chester," Julie said nervously.

"You sound like you're calling us thieves." Ricky stood up straighter. He was older and a few inches taller than Josh. His eyes had grown hard suddenly. "I told you what happened. That's the truth."

"I thought I saw that big guy from your church pick it up," said the girl wearing the in-line skates. "Isn't his name Robert or something?"

"You mean Albert Williams?" Josh asked. "He didn't take my ball. He's a friend of ours."

"So you *are* accusing us," Ricky said defiantly. "Everyone always accuses us of stuff we don't do. Those Gateway kids blame stuff on us, and now you church people are blaming us."

"Yeah," Chester echoed. "Why don't you church kids just get out of here and go back to church?"

"We only came out here today to help you all," Julie said.

"Well, I didn't ask you for no help." Ricky pointed his finger at Josh's chest. "And I didn't ask you to bring your stupid basketball. You gave it to us to play with. If I knew you were going to call me and my friends thieves just because—"

"I didn't call you thieves," Josh replied angrily. "All I'm trying to do is—"

"You sound like you're saying we're thieves." Chester took a few steps forward and stood by Ricky's side. Two other boys walked out from underneath the bridge and stood next to their friends. All four boys glared angrily at Josh and Billy. Josh took a deep breath, feeling anger and fear well up in his chest. The tension in the air was mounting.

A cry split the air. Everyone stopped talking. Over by the barbecue grill a woman was yelling.

"That's my mom!" Ricky sprinted up the creek bank and ran for his mother. Ricky's friends scrambled up the creek bank after him.

"Let's see what's going on." Josh ran after Ricky and the other kids.

By the time Josh arrived at the barbecue grill, a small crowd had gathered around Ms. Carson, who was still crying. She pulled up her apron and wiped her eyes. She had been helping serve the hamburgers and hot dogs. Pastor Brown, Julie and Carlos's father, was standing next to the upset woman.

"What's wrong?" Josh asked Chester.

"I don't know," he said with concern.

"It was right here a minute ago," Ms. Carson sobbed to Pastor Brown. "But now it's gone. Someone stole my purse, and it had my rent money in it. What am I going to do?" The woman cried again and pulled her son close to her side.

Chapter Two

Police Report

J osh gazed sympathetically at the crying woman. Her tears had caused her heavy, dark eye makeup to run down her cheeks in little black trails. Ricky reached up and wiped the smudgy black lines off his mother's cheeks.

"It's okay, Mom," Ricky said. "We'll find a way to work things out. It's okay. I'll take care of you."

Ms. Carson nodded as she sobbed and buried her head on Ricky's shoulder. The young man glared at the crowd around him as he held his mother protectively.

"What's going on?" a tall, bulky man asked as he hurried over. Everyone cleared the way for Mr. Gossett, the apartment manager. He wore black glasses and had a big black mustache. His bushy eyebrows were drawn in with a look of concern. A video camera was hanging from his neck by a strap. He had been videotaping all morning, documenting the improvements and the hard work of the people from the church.

"Apparently Ms. Carson's purse is missing," Pastor Brown said to the big man.

"It's gone, gone!" the woman sobbed. "I laid it down back on the tailgate of the pickup truck. It was right there by the ice chest. It had my rent money in it. My mother's gold necklace was in there. My driver's license. My card to the video store."

"You mean it's been stolen?" Mr. Gossett asked with a frown. He shook his head back and forth. "That's terrible. And on today of all days. It's like a party around here. Surely it's just misplaced or something. No one would steal your purse on a wonderful day like today. This is Good Friday."

"It's gone. It's gone," the short woman moaned. "I had over three hundred dollars in there. That was for rent. What am I going to do?"

"Don't you worry about the rent, Ms. Carson." The big apartment manager looked perplexed. "We'll be able to work something out."

The small woman nodded and tried to stop sobbing. She hugged her son's shoulders more tightly.

"What a day," Julie whispered to Josh. "First your basketball and now Ms. Carson's purse."

"We've got to get on this case," Billy said eagerly. "I'm telling you, there's a regular crime wave going on here, and we've got to stop it."

"I'm with you," Josh said with determination.

Pastor Brown left Ms. Carson to talk with Mr. Gossett. Julie motioned for her father to come over. He looked unhappy as he walked over.

"Who do you think is stealing things?" Julie asked her

father.

"I don't know." Pastor Brown shook his head. "It's such a shame. Jesus has been bringing hope here all day, and now the enemy is trying to rob that hope. He's the real thief in this situation."

"You think the devil stole Ms. Carson's purse?" Billy asked with surprise.

"No, not the devil himself." Pastor Brown smiled. "But God tells us our fight is not against flesh and blood but against powers and principalities, and spiritual forces of darkness. I just believe there is more going on here than someone stealing Ms. Carson's purse. We were having such a good day, but this kind of thing only brings discouragement."

"I know it makes me feel bad," Julie said. "Poor Ms. Carson."

"Yeah, and poor Josh," Billy added. "Did you hear that his brand-new basketball got stolen?"

"His father mentioned it," Pastor Brown said.

"Well, it's not as bad as Ms. Carson's problem," Josh said softly. "But I still want my ball back."

"I understand that entirely," Pastor Brown said. "I know how you feel."

"But you never had a basketball stolen," Josh grunted.

"Actually, I've had a number of things stolen or damaged over the years in the course of trying to be kind to others," Pastor Brown said.

"Really?" Josh asked in surprise.

"Sure," Pastor Brown said. "I lent my bicycle out once when I was a seminary student. The person riding my bike got hit by a car. My bicycle was destroyed, but the owner of the car bought him a new bike. He took the new bike and gave me back my ruined bike."

"He should have given you the new bike," Billy said angrily.

"That's what I thought," Pastor Brown said with a smile. "But he said the driver gave the new bike to him."

"That's a rotten deal," Josh said. "That's totally unfair."

"I've had to absorb a few other unfair deals," Pastor Brown said. "I had a slide projector borrowed and never returned. And a guitar. Several years ago when I first came to Springdale, a young man took my car without permission and then had the nerve to wreck it. Can you believe that?"

"Wow," Josh said. "Didn't that make you mad?"

"Sure," the pastor said with a crooked grin. "When something like that happens, usually I get angry. Then I have to go pray about it and ask God to help me forgive. Sometimes I have to pray quite awhile before I'm ready to make that choice. But you know Jesus said in the Sermon on the Mount to give to the one who asks to borrow and don't turn away."

"Really?" Josh asked slowly. "I guess I don't remember that being in the Bible."

"There's a number of scriptures that I sometimes wish I could forget were in the Bible." Pastor Brown winked. "But it's there, right around the part where Jesus says that if someone asks you to go a mile, go with him two miles. Or if someone strikes you on one cheek, turn the other to him also."

"I'm not letting anyone hit me and get away with it," Billy said angrily. "Are you sure Jesus said that?"

"In my Bible it's even in red letters," the pastor said with a twinkle in his eye.

"Pastor Brown!" someone called from over by the crowd of people around Ms. Carson.

"Look, the police have showed up!" Billy said excitedly. A police officer had arrived to talk to Ms. Carson.

"That's Deputy Haskins," Josh said.

"I've got to go." Pastor Brown patted Billy on the head and walked away.

The young people stood together and watched him walk over to the police officer. Josh took a deep breath and sighed.

"I still think we should try to get your ball back," Billy said. "You can't just let someone take it without doing something."

"I wish we could find Ms. Carson's purse," Emily added. "That's more serious than a missing basketball. She had over three hundred dollars stolen. That's a *real* crime."

"That's easy to say when it's not your basketball," Josh said angrily. "I mean, I'm sorry about Ms. Carson's purse too. But my basketball was brand-new."

"I think we should look for the missing purse *and* Josh's basketball," Julie said, trying to be the peacemaker. "Maybe the same person took them both."

"We don't even know what her purse looks like," Billy said.

"Well, let's go find out," Josh said.

"We're right behind you," Billy said. The six of them walked over to join the crowd of people near Ms. Carson. Deputy Haskins was writing on a clipboard. He talked to the distraught woman for almost fifteen minutes and took notes. Josh and the others waited.

"When is he ever going to finish?" Billy demanded. "The crook will be in the next county by the time he gets done writing."

"They have to follow procedures," Josh said. "You know

that."

"It takes forever," Billy said with a frown. "I want to look for clues."

"Just wait," Rebecca said to her brother. "You can't look for a stolen purse if you don't know what it looks like."

"I hate waiting," Billy replied.

"Then go get a soda and we'll wait," Rebecca said. Her brother smiled at the suggestion and ran off. Rebecca and the others laughed.

Billy had only been gone a minute when Deputy Haskins finally finished talking with Ms. Carson. He was still writing on his metal clipboard when Josh and the other young detectives walked over.

"We'd like to help look for Ms. Carson's purse," Josh said to Deputy Haskins. The police officer looked up from his writing. He smiled when he saw it was Josh. Deputy Haskins was a member of his church.

"Well, whoever took it won't have a chance if you kids get on the case," the officer said with a smile. "The Home School Detectives have a pretty good record when it comes to solving crimes."

Billy ran up holding a can of soda. He took a big gulp.

"Josh had his basketball stolen too, Deputy Haskins," Billy gasped out.

"It might not be stolen," Julie added. "We're not sure. It is missing, though."

"That's a shame." The officer continued writing. "But we'll have to take one crime at a time. You can file a report if you want. Did you have your name on your basketball?"

"No," Josh said glumly. "It was brand-new too. I should have put my name on it."

"That would have helped," Deputy Haskins said. "If some-one did take it, it would be hard to prove it was yours without your name on it."

"Well, there was a little streak of blue paint on it," Josh said. "It got on there this morning when we were painting the recreation room. That would help identify it as mine."

"That's a start," the officer said. "Do you want to file a report?"

"Maybe we should look around more first," Josh said slowly. "I mean, I'm not totally sure it was stolen. But it sure is gone."

"We think the bridge kids took it," Billy said. "But they deny it."

"Why do you think they took it?" the officer asked.

"Because they were playing with it last," Billy replied.

"Ricky Carson said they put it down by the barbecue grill when they lined up to get lunch," Julie said.

"That would put it in the same general vicinity as his mother's purse," Deputy Haskins said. "Ms. Carson said it was on the tailgate of the blue pickup truck behind the grill. She left it next to the big blue cooler that held the meat."

"What did her purse look like?" Julie asked.

"It's a small brown leather purse with a long thin brown leather strap." The police officer read off the clipboard. "She said it had over three hundred dollars in it. Some food stamps, her driver's license and house keys were also inside, as well as a gold necklace."

"Let's look around the grill," Josh said. "Maybe it's on the ground or something."

"Good luck," Deputy Haskins said.

Eddie Reeser, the part-time maintenance man, was taking

the last few hamburgers off the grill when Josh and the other kids walked over. Eddie was tall and thin and wore a sleeveless T-shirt. A red-and-white checked apron was tied around his waist. His bare arms were strong and muscled, with a large tattoo of a bear on his left shoulder. An eagle tattoo perched on his right shoulder. Dark sunglasses were propped up above his forehead. His thick black hair was slicked back.

"Hey, Josh," Eddie said with a smile. "You guys want more burgers? I got a few good ones left. A couple are all dried out and burnt. I'm going to eat those."

"No, Eddie," Josh said. "We came to look for Ms. Carson's purse."

"Yeah, I've been looking too," Eddie said. "I saw her put it down. But when everyone lined up to get burgers, it got kind of confusing around here. We had lots of customers passing by really fast. When the line was almost done and she went to get more burgers, she saw that it was missing."

"Where was it?" Josh asked.

"Just back there on the tailgate of Mr. Gordan's pickup truck," Eddie said. "It was right next to the cooler where we kept all the raw hamburger patties and hot dogs."

"That's one of our coolers," Emily Morgan said.

"You didn't see anyone hanging around back there, did you?" Josh asked.

"Not really." Eddie shook his head sadly. "But like I said, we all got real busy once people lined up. This is really a shame. Here everyone is doing such good things today, all you church people cleaning stuff up and making this old place look good. You guys sure made my job a lot easier. I was way behind on helping people keep things fixed up. This is the best day in the history of this place, and then someone starts stealing. Some people are just mean."

"They sure are," Josh agreed.

"Josh's basketball got stolen," Billy said.

"Yeah, I heard it was missing." Eddie nodded sadly. "That's a shame too. I saw some of them shooting hoops with it. I was wanting to take a break and shoot a few myself. It looked like a nice ball."

"A real leather cover too, like in the pros." Josh doubled his fists, wishing he had something to hit.

"We wondered if some of the bridge kids took it," Billy said. "Maybe you could ask a few questions for us. You're a big guy. They'd be afraid of you."

"Billy!" Rebecca said.

"That's okay." Eddie smiled at Billy's comments. "So you think I'm tough?"

"You look tough," Billy replied. "You're the only person I know with tattoos."

"Billy!" Rebecca repeated. "Don't say that."

"Hey, I am tough," Eddie said with a smile. Josh couldn't tell if Eddie was serious or not.

"Your tattoos look real . . . uh, nice . . ." Julie said uncomfortably.

"Nice?" Eddie asked. She couldn't tell if he was insulted or not.

"I mean . . . uh . . . professionally done. That's what I mean," Julie said.

"Yeah, very professional," Emily added and smiled.

"Well, I think he did a good job for a guy who was halfway drunk," Eddie said with a lopsided grin. "Of course, I wouldn't have let him if I hadn't been in worse shape myself. I'm scared of those needles."

"You were drunk?" Emily asked.

"I was in a bad way for sure," Eddie said, nodding his head. "I personally don't recommend it, I mean, getting a tattoo at your age."

"I'm not getting a tattoo," Emily said with surprise.

"Mom and Dad wouldn't let her," Josh added with a grin. "They hardly even let her get her ears pierced."

"Some girls like 'em," Eddie said. "But tattoos hurt plenty. I remember that. I hated that buzzing sound and those little needles. Anyway, that was a few years ago. I was working as a sound man for a rock band back then, up in Minnesota. Lots of guys in the band had tattoos. Including Melinda, the lead singer. She had about four or more. I do like the way they look, I guess." He flexed the biceps on his arms to spread the tattoos out wider.

"Of course, I look tougher when I'm not wearing an apron." Eddie held up the edge of the apron as if it were a skirt. He reached around, untied it and hung it over the back of a chair.

"Do you think you could talk to the bridge kids about Josh's basketball?" Billy asked. "I mean, you know them better than we do."

"Sure, I could ask them." Eddie reached down and got a cigarette out of a pack lying near the grill. He bent over the grill and stuck the tip of the cigarette on a coal. He leaned back and puffed. "Man, I've been dying for a smoke for a half hour. Of course, I don't recommend you kids take up smoking either. You're still too young, even though I know lots of kids around here smoke."

"I don't want to smoke," Josh said.

"Yeah, it's a bad habit and really expensive." Eddie blew

out a big stream of smoke. "I'd hate to think how much money I've spent on cigarettes. I've tried to quit. But I've been smoking a long time. Since your age, I bet. I started when I was twelve and now I'm twenty-two. That's ten years of cigarettes. That's a lot of smokes, you know?"

"You started smoking at age twelve?" Billy said. "I'm surprised you aren't dead by now."

"Billy!" Rebecca moaned, rolling her eyes.

"What?" Billy said. "It says right there on cigarette packs about the Surgeon General saying it's harmful to your health and can kill you."

"That surgeon knows what he's talking about," Eddie said. "You kids don't want to be smoking at your age. You'd spend all your allowance real quick. Well, I was going to clean this stuff up. Then maybe I can help you look for your basketball."

The tall tattooed man walked behind the grill and picked up the blue ice chest.

"This belongs to someone in your church," Eddie said.

"That goes in our van," Josh said. "I'll show you the way. It should be unlocked."

Eddie's muscles bulged as he carried the cooler. The cigarette was clamped firmly in his lips.

Josh and the others walked in front of Eddie to the Morgan's van, which was parked under a tree. Josh opened the back doors of the van. A big orange cooler was packed in the back, along with a tool box and a black guitar case.

"Hey, who plays the guitar?" Eddie asked eagerly as he set the blue cooler down on top of the orange cooler.

"It's mine," Josh said, feeling flattered that Eddie was impressed.

"That's really great," Eddie said. "It's good to be musical

at your age."

"We all play," Carlos said eagerly. "We have a musical group."

"A regular band, huh?" Eddie said. "That's super."

"I play drums when they let me," Billy added eagerly.

"I bet you're a great drummer," Eddie said. "I can play the harmonica. I used to play a few numbers with a band once."

"The one in Minnesota?" Julie asked.

"No, this was when I lived in Cleveland," Eddie replied. "It was a kind of blues band. I did some vocals and played the harp."

"You played a harp?" Emily asked in disbelief.

"Yeah, the harp," Eddie said. "Not the big kind with all the strings, but the harmonica. We called them harps too."

"Wow!" Billy said.

"We were pretty good, but Nick, the leader of the group, decided to get married and get a job with a computer firm," Eddie said. "I don't blame him. We weren't making enough money to really survive. The music business is a rough place to make a buck, let me tell you. One time we—"

"Do you think you could go talk to those guys about my basketball?" Josh interrupted, trying not to act as impatient as he felt.

"Yeah, sure. I know all the kids around here, and even half the ones at Gateway 'cause they hang out around here by the bridge." Eddie threw the cigarette butt down.

"What's that?" Emily pointed to Josh's guitar case.

"What's what?" Josh asked.

"That cord coming out of your case?" Emily pointed at a brown rope. Josh looked where she pointed. He squinted. A small loop of thin brown cord was sticking out of the neck of

Josh's guitar case.

"Don't look like a cord for an amplifier," Eddie said.

"I don't know what it is," Josh said.

"Let's see," Billy said.

Josh undid the snaps on his guitar case. He lifted the lid. They all saw it at the same time. Buried down underneath the guitar's neck was a dark brown something. Josh lifted the guitar up so he could get to it. Billy reached forward and grabbed the brown cord and pulled. Everyone just stared. A brown leather purse dangled back and forth from Billy's hand.

"Hey, that looks just like Ms. Carson's purse." Eddie frowned, turned and looked at Josh with a puzzled face.

Emily opened the purse. She reached inside and opened a wallet.

"The driver's license says Judy Carson," Emily said softly.

"We found the stolen purse!" Billy said with excitement. "But what's it doing in your guitar case, Josh?"

Everyone looked at Josh curiously. Josh stared at the brown purse. He looked at the questioning faces of his friends, but he didn't know what to say.

Chapter Three

Josh Accused

I don't know how it got there." Josh stared at the purse.
"Josh, your face is really getting red," Billy said
curiously.

"Shut up!" Josh muttered.

"Josh, how did that purse get in your guitar case?" Emily
asked softly.

"I don't know," Josh repeated. "I have no idea. I didn't put
it there."

"But you guys sure found it," Eddie said with an uneasy
smile. "When they said you guys were detectives, I wasn't
sure whether to believe them or not, but you guys really found
that purse fast. Let's go take it to Judy."

Eddie grabbed the purse and walked away. Josh watched
him go. He looked at his open guitar case as if he'd seen a
ghost.

"Let's go follow Eddie!" Billy took off after the maintenance man.

"Yeah, we better," Josh said. "Hey, Eddie, wait up. Wait!"

Josh ran after Billy. All the others left except Emily, who carefully closed the guitar case and shut the back door of the van.

"Judy, we found your purse!" Eddie held it up by the barbecue grill. Josh and Billy ran up behind him. Ricky and his friends ran over. Deputy Haskins walked up with a smile. Mr. Gossett joined the group as well.

"My purse!" the single mom yelled with glee.

"You got it back," Ricky said with a smile. "Way to go."

"The Home School Detectives found it," Eddie said.

Ms. Carson snatched the brown leather bag out of Eddie's hand. She quickly opened it and took out her wallet. She flipped it open. Her smile turned to a frown.

"Where's the money?" she asked. "My driver's license is here. But my money is gone. All my cash. It's still gone. And the necklace is missing."

"Sorry," Eddie said. "I thought maybe it would be there since . . ."

"Where did you find it?"

"It was in Josh Morgan's guitar case," Billy said. "Isn't that an odd place for it to turn up?"

"Billy!" Josh whispered.

"Well, that's where we found it," Billy said defensively.

"In Josh's guitar case?" Ricky frowned and turned to Josh.

"I didn't put it there," Josh said.

"How come my mom's purse is in your guitar case if you didn't put it there?" Ricky demanded. "And what happened to her money and necklace?"

"I tell you, I don't know," Josh repeated. His face felt very hot and was getting hotter by the second. The whole world seemed to be staring at him. Pastor Brown had joined the crowd as well as many others. News spread quickly about the missing purse being found.

"My money is still gone," Ms. Carson moaned. She showed the wallet to Deputy Haskins. The police officer looked and nodded. Then he turned to Josh.

"You didn't put it in your guitar case?" Deputy Haskins asked.

"Of course not." Josh knew his face was bright red. "I never even saw it until we found it a minute ago."

"I'm missing over three hundred dollars and my mother's necklace." Ms. Carson began to sob again. Ricky moved closer to his mother and hugged her. He glared at Josh.

"I'm telling you, I didn't put it there, and I don't have three hundred dollars or her necklace," Josh said. The crowd of faces all looked at Josh quietly.

"You're accusing me of being the thief of your stupid basketball, and it turns out you're the one taking things," Ricky said bitterly.

"But I didn't take it," Josh said with anger and fear in his voice.

"Then why was it in your guitar case?" Ricky asked loudly. He looked over at Chester, who nodded and stared at Josh with distrust.

"Yeah!" Chester taunted. "Here he was a little while ago accusing us of taking his basketball, which we didn't. But now Ms. Carson's lost purse turns up in his guitar case. Are you going to arrest him, Deputy Haskins?"

"I'm not making any arrests," Deputy Haskins said firmly. "We need more facts."

"Why not?" Ricky asked. "If you had found that purse in the guitar case in Chester's apartment I bet you would arrest him. A week ago the police were out here, and Mr. Gossett wanted them to arrest us all for that dumpster that caught on fire in the parking lot."

"You weren't the only suspects in that case," the police officer said.

"I bet those Gateway guys did it," Chester said. "But people around here act like we did it."

"Yeah, those Gateway kids probably started that fire," Ricky said. "Then they blamed us."

"That fire is still under investigation," Deputy Haskins said firmly. "No one has been charged with setting it."

"Well, thankfully the fire didn't spread," Mr. Gossett said. "It could have caused a lot of damage. What if the trees caught on fire, or the apartment building?"

"None of us did it," Ricky insisted.

"Well, that trash didn't catch on fire by itself," Mr. Gossett replied. "Just like that purse didn't get in Josh's guitar case in the van by itself."

"But I'm telling you, I didn't put it there." Josh wanted to scream at all the staring faces. "The van wasn't locked. Anyone could have put it in there."

"Yeah, he didn't have to unlock the van," Eddie said. "I'm a witness to that, Deputy. The van was open."

"Someone else put it there," Josh said. "I know it looks suspicious, but I didn't do it. Things aren't always what they seem to be."

"That's right," Billy added energetically. "We know all about that. Just a month ago, they accused Josh of stealing baseball cards at the grocery store."

"You stole baseball cards too?" Mr. Gossett looked at Josh with a frown on his very big face.

"I didn't steal any baseball cards." Josh rolled his eyes as he looked at Billy.

"If you didn't steal them, why did they say you did?" Ricky demanded.

"Yeah, they accused my oldest brother of stealing a pack of meat," Chester said. "He got in a lot of trouble."

"Look, I didn't steal anything," Josh said, trying to sound calm, though his voice cracked. A lump was in his throat. "It was all a big mistake. We were in the grocery store. I was going to buy two packs of baseball cards. I got the cards and took them with me to the magazine stand inside the store. I was going to buy a guitar magazine. I had put the cards down on the magazine shelf. I was looking through the magazine when my mother called for us to go. I put the magazine down on the shelf and followed her outside because she was in a hurry. The store detective followed me out. He thought I had put the cards in my pocket."

"Caught you red handed, eh?" Chester asked. "Those store detectives are smart. My brother found that out."

"No, he didn't catch me," Josh said with frustration.

"You mean you got away with it?" Ricky asked cynically.

"I didn't get away with anything because I didn't steal anything," Josh said. "I had put the baseball cards on the magazine shelf, and when I put down the magazine, I put it down on top of the baseball cards so the store detective didn't see them, and he assumed I took them."

"Yeah, Josh was totally innocent," Billy said to Ricky and his friends. "It was all a big mistake. The store detective apologized when Josh went back inside and showed him the baseball cards underneath the magazine."

"Yeah, well that doesn't explain how my mother's purse got in your guitar case," Ricky spat out. "Her money is missing. I think you need to search him, Deputy Haskins. See if he's got the money on him."

"I haven't got any money." Josh pulled out his front pockets. "And I didn't put your mom's purse in my guitar case."

The crowd of people stared at Josh's empty pants pockets. Deputy Haskins looked at Josh, who was very red in the face.

"Let's settle down, folks," the police officer said. "People are innocent until proven guilty. We need to get more facts in this case."

"Some people think you're guilty whether they have facts or not," Ricky said cynically.

"Let's have a talk, Josh," the officer said.

"Sure." Josh followed the police officer away from the crowd. They stopped under a tree. The officer opened his clipboard and looked down at his form. Josh waited nervously. The police officer then looked up at Josh. He smiled.

"Rough day, huh?" the police officer said.

"I can't believe this is happening," Josh said. "First my basketball gets stolen, and now they're accusing me of stealing Ms. Carson's money."

"Well, it doesn't look good, Josh," the officer said. "You know if you did take something, the sooner you give it back, the better it goes. She might not press charges."

"I don't have anything to give back." Josh's voice cracked. For a moment he was afraid he was going to cry, but he forced himself not to. He wondered if crying would make him look more guilty or more innocent. He didn't want to cry. The whole day had suddenly become a nightmare. "I promise you, I did not take Ms. Carson's purse. I didn't. I don't know how it got there. In fact, I think I've been with my friends the whole time I've been here today. You can ask them. We've been working together all day."

"You all have done a lot of good work." The police officer nodded as he looked around. "You've made this place look two hundred percent better, according to Mr. Gossett. I've never seen him so happy. What did you do today?"

"When we first got here, I worked on the flower bed, helping pull weeds," Josh said. "Then later I helped carry junk and stuff out of that spare room on the first floor near the washing machines and dryers. They are making it into a recreation room. I helped paint in there too. Carlos was with me."

"Mr. Gossett donated a Ping-Pong table for that room," the police officer said. "That was a nice thing."

"Yeah," Josh said. "There are board games and other stuff in there too. Mr. Samuel's apartment is right across the hall. He's going to watch it and open it up after school. Since he's retired, he can keep an eye on things. Mr. Gossett said he was afraid people might steal stuff."

"Mr. Gossett wants to put a soda machine in there now too," the officer said. "Sometimes people try to break into those machines."

"Stealing messes up things for everyone," Josh said sadly.

"It sure does." The police officer looked at Josh silently.

"I didn't take that purse," Josh said. "Someone must have taken her purse and taken the money and just hid it there."

"Maybe," the police officer said. "Your van was unlocked?"

"I think they left it open so people from the church could get to my dad's tool box if they needed to use a tool," Josh said. "I don't understand why someone would stick the purse in my guitar case."

"Well, when we found out her purse was missing, I had people check in the dumpster and behind the bushes along the sidewalk," Deputy Haskins said. "Most thieves would take a thing like a purse, get the money out and throw the purse away quickly."

"They could have dumped it in our van instead," Josh said. "Like just opening the door and stuffing it in there."

"That's possible," the officer said. "I would think that a thief in a hurry would just shove it under the seat. It's odd that they took the trouble to put it in your guitar case."

"Well, I promise you, I didn't put it there," Josh said. "Don't you believe me?"

The officer looked at Josh without speaking. He closed up his clipboard and put the pen away.

"Yes, I do believe you," the police officer said. "I know you, Josh. And I believe what you say. I think the thief probably got inside the van and ducked down so he or she could go through the purse without being noticed. Then he stuck it in the guitar case to hide it so it wouldn't be discovered right away."

"I'm sorry her money is missing," Josh said. "Three hundred dollars is a lot of money."

"What's worse, Josh, is that it looks like you took it," the police officer said. "A good reputation based on true character is priceless. Once it's tainted, it's hard to restore, believe me. When your basketball turned up missing, you assumed it was the kids out here who took it, right?"

"Well, they had it last," Josh said slowly.

"That's what we call circumstantial evidence," the officer said. "In this circumstance, they were the last ones to have your ball. Therefore, you would naturally assume they were the ones responsible for it. And when it turned up missing, you assumed they took it."

"Well, it looks that way," Josh said.

"Just like it looks bad for you when Ms. Carson's purse turns up in your guitar case," the officer said.

"But that's different," Josh said. "I mean, everyone knows about the kids out here. I mean, people out here . . . they have reputations for causing . . ."

"Some people out here have bad reputations for causing trouble," the officer said. "So if something bad happens around here, they suspect the bridge kids. A few rotten apples can spoil the whole barrel, right?"

"Well, yeah," Josh said. "Of course, they might not have done it . . . I mean, I guess I suspected them because . . ."

"Because there are problems on this side of town," the police officer said. "In times like this, you can see what your reputation means. Right now there's a big cloud of suspicion over you. People who don't know you like I do may actually think you're a thief. The circumstances don't look good, do they?"

"I guess not," Josh said softly. "But I'm not a thief. It may look bad, but I still didn't do it."

Just then, Josh saw his mother and father coming across the parking lot toward him. Pastor Brown was with them. Josh's parents looked very serious as they walked up.

"We heard there was a problem," Mr. Morgan said to Deputy Haskins.

"Dad, it's been horrible." Josh quickly blurted out about his missing basketball and then finding the purse in his guitar case. Deputy Haskins filled in the rest of the story. Mr. and Mrs. Morgan listened attentively. Mr. Morgan had his arm around Josh. He gave him a big hug when the police officer finished talking.

"And your basketball got stolen too?" Mr. Morgan asked.

"Yes." Josh felt his voice crack again, and he knew he was going to cry. He buried his face in his father's shoulder. He hoped no one was watching, but he couldn't help himself.

"I didn't do it. I didn't do it," Josh cried.

"I believe you, Josh," his father said.

"And so do I," Deputy Haskins said.

Josh wiped his eyes with his sleeve. Over by the barbecue pit, he could see his sister and his other friends watching him. Josh turned away and wiped his eyes again with his arm. His mother handed him a tissue from her purse. He blew his nose and felt better. His mom smiled sympathetically.

"I was just telling Josh that it's at a time like this when your reputation really counts," the police officer said.

"Yeah, but what good is it when other people think you are a thief?" Josh asked angrily. "I can say I didn't take that money, but I can't prove it."

"Well, in a way you can't, and that will leave a cloud of suspicion hanging over you," the officer said. "Some people will still think you're guilty. The only sure way to clear you of suspicion is to catch the person who really did take Ms. Carson's purse and stole her money."

"That's right!" Josh said. "If we can find the real thief, then no one can say I did it. I'll be in the clear for sure!"

"Sounds like the Home School Detectives have their next

case," Mr. Morgan said, patting Josh on the shoulder.

"Yeah," Josh said with determination. "This is one case we have to solve. I want my name cleared."

"Well, I wouldn't get your hopes up too high," the police officer said. "Thefts like this can be awfully hard to solve."

"Deputy Haskins is right, Josh," his father said.

"But we have to solve it," Josh replied. "It's my reputation. And it's worth a lot more than three hundred dollars. Can I go now?" Josh looked into the eyes of the police officer.

"You're perfectly free, Josh," Deputy Haskins replied.

"I don't feel free," Josh said. "Not until we catch the real thief. I'm not going to stop until we find out without a doubt who did this. I have to know."

Chapter Four

Under the
Broken Bridge

Josh's friends waited for him by his family's van. He
walked over slowly. He hoped his eyes didn't look too
red.

"Are they taking you to jail?" Billy asked carefully.

"Of course not," Josh grunted. "I didn't take that money."

"I know you didn't. I was just praying that Deputy Haskins believed you," Billy said. "Ricky and his mom and Mr.
Gossett weren't very nice. You should have heard the stuff
they were saying after you left."

"Well, it didn't help for you to mention that stuff about the
baseball cards," Josh said angrily. "Why in the world did you
bring that up?"

"Because it seemed like the same kind of misunderstand-
ing," Billy said. "I was just trying to help."

"It made it worse, Billy," Carlos said.

"Yeah," Julie agreed.

"That's right, Billy," Rebecca added. "It's like Mom and Dad say: you need to think about ten seconds before you open your mouth when you get excited."

"But I didn't mean any harm," Billy said. "The store detective said he made a mistake that time. That just shows how misunderstandings can happen."

"Well, it just added to the confusion and made things worse," Josh said. "You made it sound like I actually stole those baseball cards."

"I'm sorry," Billy said defensively. He looked at the accusing faces of his friends. "I was only trying to help."

"What are we going to do?" Carlos asked.

"We *have* to find the real thief of Ms. Carson's purse," Josh said seriously. "If we catch the real thief, then people will quit thinking I took the money."

"Maybe one of the bridge kids took her purse too," Billy offered. "They might have taken your ball, and then, to make things worse, they might have tried to set it up so it looked like you stole Ms. Carson's purse."

"But why would they do that?" Emily asked.

"Maybe they don't like Josh," Billy said.

"That's possible, but what has Josh ever done to any of them to make them mad?" Julie asked.

"Nothing," Josh said. "I've never had any trouble with any of those guys. In fact, the second time we came over here, I helped Ricky and Chester with their schoolwork."

"You did?" Emily asked with surprise. "You didn't tell me that."

"When Dad and Pastor Brown were here last week talking

with Mr. Gossett and Eddie about fixing things up, I got to talking with Ricky and Chester," Josh said. "They were doing their math homework out in the hallway together. It was stuff we've already studied. I offered to help and showed them a few things, that's all. They had a test the next day and were scared to go to school."

"You helped those guys, and then they stole your basketball?" Billy asked. "That's really ungrateful."

"Maybe they didn't take my ball," Josh said slowly.

"But you thought they were the chief suspects before," Billy protested.

"Well, at first I thought they did take it," Josh said. "Now I'm not sure."

"I thought you all were being too quick to judge," Julie said. "Now Ricky and his friends are mad at us because you accused them of stealing the ball."

"I don't blame them," Emily said.

"I guess I don't blame them either," Josh added slowly.

"What?" Billy asked in disbelief. "But they're the prime suspects. Everybody knows their reputation."

"Well, maybe they don't deserve that reputation," Josh said. "Things aren't always the way they seem on the surface. Besides, people are innocent until proven guilty."

"Like you," Emily said.

"Yeah," Josh said. "You don't know what it feels like to have everyone thinking you're a thief."

"Well, let's find the real thief then," Billy said. "We've got to clear Josh's name."

"We need to pick up trash first," Josh replied.

"Pick up trash?" Billy asked in disbelief. "You're kidding."

"That's right," Carlos said. "I forgot. We promised we

would pick up trash around the building after we ate lunch, didn't we?"

"The bags are in the van." Josh walked over to the rear of the van and opened the doors. A box of green plastic garbage bags was behind the coolers. He pulled out two bags and stuffed one in the hip pocket of his jeans.

"I don't see why we have to pick up trash when we have an important case to solve," Billy said unhappily. "Besides, it's boring."

"We need to keep our word to Mr. Gossett and the others," Josh said. "We said we'd do it, and we need to follow through."

"But Mr. Gossett doesn't even trust you," Billy said.

"That's all the more reason we need to do what we promised," Josh said. "To show him that we're people who keep our word. I want to prove to him that he's wrong about me, that I am trustworthy. And one way you do that is by keeping your word."

"Josh is right," Julie agreed.

"But we shouldn't have to prove anything to anyone," Billy said angrily. "We've already helped out here a lot. Isn't that enough?"

"Not until we do all we said we would do." Josh gave the box of trash bags to Billy, who took one. He gave the box to Carlos. Josh watched as everyone got at least one bag. "If we said we'd do it, we have to do it."

"We can still keep our eyes and ears open for clues," Carlos said excitedly.

"That's right," Emily said. "You know, later, Mr. Gossett said there was another person he suspected, but he didn't mention any names. He said he'd talk to the police."

"I wish he'd give us a hint," Billy said. "We need all the clues we can get."

"Well, let's see what we can find out while we clean up," Josh said. "I'll take the creek bed and under the old bridge. The rest of you can spread out."

"I still think this is a mistake," Billy said despondently. "Picking up trash is so boring."

Josh walked over to the creek, thankful to be alone. He climbed carefully down into the creek bed. Lots of trash had collected down in the creek and on the banks. Old cans, bottles, plastic bags, paper cups and bits of paper littered the bottom and sides of the mostly dry creek. Josh was careful as he picked things up. He knew from past painful experiences that ants or other biting insects could be hiding in or on pieces of trash.

He worked his way slowly up the creek bed toward the old broken bridge. Being by himself gave Josh time to think. He thought that he should pray. He wanted to pray that his name would be cleared, but it was hard. He was worried about it. But the more Josh tried to pray, the more he kept thinking about his missing basketball and how he had accused the bridge kids of stealing it. Thinking about that made him feel bad, but he wasn't sure why.

"They probably did take it," Josh said, feeling a surge of anger. But all he could think of was how angry Ricky had looked. He and Chester had been ready to fight about it.

Josh started to round a bend in the creek when he heard voices. One of them sounded familiar. He put down his plastic bag. He peered through some tall grass. Around the bend, Ricky Carson was talking to a man with long hair and long sideburns and big brown cowboy boots. Ricky held a big brown manila envelope in his hands. He gave the envelope to the man.

"That's all I have from this week," Ricky said.

The man took the envelope and smiled. He pulled a white envelope from his back pocket and gave it to Ricky. "And that's what I have," the long-haired man said.

Ricky opened the envelope. Josh could see the green color of cash. "Good week," Ricky said with a smile.

"Hard work pays off, just like I told you," the man said with a grin. He tapped Ricky on top of his head with the big brown envelope.

"Do you want a hamburger or hot dog?" Ricky asked.

"No way." The man pulled his hair back. "If they see my face around here, I'll be in trouble. I'll be in touch. In the meantime, I want the next batch as soon as you're ready."

The man smiled again, turned and then walked up over the opposite creek bank, out of sight. Ricky watched him go. Then he stuck the white envelope with the money in his back pocket. He looked around to see if anyone was watching.

Josh ducked down behind a large bush. He waited for a long minute. He was almost certain that Ricky had seen him. He kept waiting to hear Ricky's voice accusing him of spying. But the accusations were only in Josh's head. After two minutes of endless waiting, Josh peeked up over the bush. Ricky was gone.

Josh picked up his plastic bag and continued around the bend in the creek bed. He wondered why Ricky was receiving money from the strange man and what he had given in exchange to get it. Apparently the man thought he would be in trouble if others saw him. But why? Maybe they were meeting in the creek because Deputy Haskins was nearby.

Maybe the man was hiding from the police. Josh wondered if he should go tell Deputy Haskins. But what would he tell? He picked up more and more trash, letting the questions run over and over in his mind. His bag was almost full as he got near the old broken bridge.

Josh was relieved that neither Ricky nor any of the other kids were under the old broken bridge. The place was littered with paper, plastic, and empty soda and beer cans.

Josh quickly filled up the first sack and tied the top off and started filling the second green sack. He was constantly bent over, picking up the litter off the ground. He moved into the shadow beneath the old wooden bridge. Speckles of light came through the old loose boards above him. He stopped to straighten his back and to look at the spray-painted messages on the old bridge. The bridge had been painted so many times that it was hard to read any single message or word since there were different colors and signs on top of each other. The big blue cross stood out among all the rest. No one had painted on top of it. He wondered if Jesus would be happy that his name and a picture of the cross were painted on the bridge among all the graffiti.

"It's too bad they wrote your name the wrong way," Josh said softly. He was surprised at his own thoughts. He spoke as if Jesus were right there under the bridge. But would Jesus hang around the same place as kids with bad reputations? Josh wondered what Jesus thought of the bridge kids. He bent down and headed further under the bridge. There were lots of empty beer cans lying on the ground. He picked them up quickly.

"Are you stealing our stuff?" a voice asked.

Josh jumped at the sound. He turned around. Several boys

were standing at one end of the bridge behind him. He didn't recognize any of the faces. He was sure it would be Ricky or Chester or his friends. The tall boy in front wore a long, dirty, white T-shirt. He held a can of spray paint in his hand. Four other boys were behind him.

"I'm just picking up trash," Josh said.

"You're trespassing," the taller boy said.

"I'm just picking up trash," Josh repeated.

"How do we know that?" the taller boy asked. "Check it out, Antonio."

A stocky Hispanic boy stepped forward. He walked toward Josh without smiling. He picked up the full sack of trash and undid the tie.

"It's just trash," Josh said firmly.

"Let me check." Antonio turned the bag upside down and all the trash Josh had picked up came spilling out under the bridge. He let the empty garbage bag drop to the ground. "It's garbage, Mike."

Josh stared at the pile of litter on the ground. He took a deep breath, trying to control his anger. He suddenly realized that he was afraid as well as being angry. The taller boy named Mike walked toward him.

"You're new here," the taller boy said. "You Bridgewood kids need to learn to keep off Gateway property."

"I don't live in Bridgewood," Josh said.

"Then what are you doing here?"

"I'm with the Springdale Community Church," Josh said. "We've been helping the people out here clean things up."

"So that's what the party is about," the taller boy said. "Why didn't they invite us?"

"You live at the Gateway Apartments?" Josh asked.

"Yes. Is there something wrong with that?"

"No," Josh said. "I didn't say that. If you want to know why you weren't invited, you can go ask Pastor Brown or Mr. Gossett. Or Deputy Haskins of the police department. They're all close by. I can call them if you want."

"Relax, Trash Boy," Mike said. "We just want to know what's going on and why all these people are around."

"Look, I'm just trying to help out here by picking up trash."

"You're saying our bridge and creek are messy?" Mike asked. "You don't think we keep things beautiful?"

Josh looked the taller boy in the eyes. Then he looked at his friends. They were all staring at him with glinting, hard eyes.

"I'm saying there's a lot of trash in this creek bed and under the bridge," Josh replied. "And I am here to pick it up. That's what I'm doing. When I'm done, it probably won't look beautiful, but maybe it will look better."

Josh bent down and put some more beer cans in the sack he was holding. He wasn't sure what would happen next. The taller boy watched him with some surprise. Then his face turned sour. Only he wasn't looking at Josh, but behind him. Josh turned around.

Ricky and Chester and several other Bridgewood kids ran down the creek bank behind Josh on the other side of the bridge. Mike's sour look changed to fear. Josh looked back and forth between Ricky and Mike, who were staring silently at each other. He felt like he was going to be in the middle of a very big fight very soon.

"Next time, I want to be invited to the party," Mike said softly. He backed up and joined his friends. They backed away from under the bridge. Then they turned and ran up the opposite creek bank.

Josh took a deep breath. He looked over at Ricky and the others and gave a half-hearted smile.

"I'm glad you guys showed up," Josh said uncomfortably.

"Those Gateway kids giving you a hard time?" Ricky asked angrily.

"They dumped my trash out, that's all." Josh pointed at the pile of litter on the ground. He picked up the empty bag and began stuffing the trash back inside the bag.

"They act tough, but they're all a bunch of chickens," Ricky said.

"Mike had a can of spray paint," Josh said. "He acted like he wanted to use me as a canvas."

"He can't even spell his name he's so stupid," Chester said. "That boy is never going to finish the ninth grade."

The other kids laughed. Then they got quiet again as they watched Josh picking up the trash. Josh could feel their stares. He wasn't sure what they were thinking. When he had finished picking up all the trash that Antonio had dumped out, he tied the bag up again with a new tie. Josh then picked up the other bag he had been filling when the Gateway kids first arrived.

"You look like those guys that work out on the interstate highway picking up trash," Chester observed.

"I guess," Josh replied. He wasn't sure what to say. Then almost without thinking, he turned to Ricky.

"Look, I'm sorry for accusing you guys of stealing my basketball," Josh blurted out quickly. "I shouldn't have done that. I was upset because that ball is brand-new. But it wasn't right. So I'm sorry. Please forgive me."

Ricky and Chester and the others just stared at Josh without speaking. Ricky looked surprised.

"We told you where we left your ball," Ricky said finally.

"I know." Josh looked him in the eye. "Somebody else must have taken it. Somebody is stealing stuff around here. I know you guys probably don't believe me since your mom's purse turned up in my guitar case, but I promise you all, I had nothing to do with that. I don't know how it got there."

"We don't know what to believe," Chester said suspiciously. "But your friends Billy and Carlos want to see you. They said for us to tell you to come right away."

"What's wrong?" Josh asked.

"The thief struck again," Ricky said. "Mr. Gossett just found out his video camera is missing. It happened just a little while ago. Your friends want to talk to you. They say they may have a clue—"

Josh didn't wait to hear the rest. He had already started running out from underneath the old bridge.

Chapter Five

The Bridgewood Thief

As he neared the crowd gathered out in the parking lot, Josh remembered that he had left his bags of litter under the bridge. He slowed down, about to go back and get them, when he saw Pastor Brown and Deputy Haskins talking to Mr. Gossett. Ms. Carson was standing next to Mr. Gossett. Billy and Carlos waved for Josh to come over. Josh decided he could go back later to pick up the trash bags.

"Someone stole Mr. Gossett's camera," Billy said. "I told Ricky to find you."

"When did he discover it was missing?" Josh asked.

"Just a few minutes ago," Carlos said. "He is really angry. But at least he knows it wasn't you. Apparently someone took it while you were talking about Ms. Carson's purse with Deputy Haskins."

"He said he put the camera in his office in the apartment building," Billy said. "Deputy Haskins is getting the names of the people who were still working inside, to see if they saw anything. Some people were painting the hallway on that floor."

"This is turning out to be a really bad day for people stealing stuff," Josh said.

"Mr. Gossett is really mad," Billy said.

Josh looked over at the big man, whose face was red with anger. He moved closer to the crowd to hear what he was saying.

"Luckily I have my tape," Mr. Gossett said, holding up a small eight-millimeter videotape. "At least the thief didn't get that. I only wish we had security cameras around here to help keep an eye on things. All the new apartments have modern security equipment. We obviously need some help around here."

He waved the tape around for the other people to see. When he saw Josh, the big man frowned. He glared at Josh for an instant and then turned back to Deputy Haskins.

"I don't think we are wanted around here," Josh said softly. "Let's give him some room." Josh walked over to his family's van. Carlos and Billy were right on his heels. Josh tried to open the back of the van, but it was locked. He stood on his tiptoes and looked down through the rear window.

"I just wanted to make sure my guitar was still there," Josh said. "You never know what might happen around this place."

"Yeah, it's a really weird feeling," Billy said. "The whole time I was picking up trash, I kept checking my back pocket to make sure my wallet was still there."

"Do you have any money in it?" Carlos asked.

"Just a dollar," Billy said. "But I don't want the Bridge-wood thief walking off with it."

"The Bridgewood thief?" Josh asked.

"That's what some of the people around here are calling him," Carlos said. "As I was picking up trash, I listened to people talking, you know, listening for clues."

"I may have a clue," Josh said.

"What's that?"

"I saw Ricky Carson get some kind of payoff in the creek bed," Josh replied.

"A payoff?" Billy asked. "What do you mean?"

Josh quickly told them about seeing Ricky and the man exchanging envelopes.

"And you're sure it was money in the envelope he gave to Ricky?" Carlos asked.

"I saw it with my own eyes," Josh said.

"I wonder what was in the big envelope." Billy said. "Maybe it was drugs. I bet it was something illegal."

"I don't know," Josh said. "It seemed pretty flat. I do know that the man he was talking to didn't want to be seen. I heard him say that."

Emily, Julie and Rebecca walked across the parking lot holding half-full sacks of trash. They headed straight for the van. They dropped their trash bags with looks of relief.

"We have news," Rebecca said with a grin.

"So does Josh," Billy replied excitedly. "You heard about Mr. Gossett's video camera being stolen, didn't you?"

"Of course," Emily said. "All the older people who live around here are talking about it. But you'll never guess who some of them suspect."

"Who?"

"Eddie Reeser," Julie said. "I heard Mr. Samuel tell Mrs. Perkins and Mrs. May that he had heard Eddie and Mr. Gossett arguing over money in the hallway last week. They said Eddie was really mad. They said he even threatened Mr. Gossett, that if he wasn't paid soon, Mr. Gossett would be sorry."

"Really?" Josh asked with interest. "That may fit. I wondered about Eddie earlier. You know he was around Ms. Carson's purse more than we were. Plus he was the one who took the cooler to the back of the van. He knew the van was open. He could have taken her purse, gotten the money, slipped it into my guitar case, and no one would have noticed. Then he made sure that we discovered it. He could be the one we're looking for."

"As a maintenance man he must have access keys to all the locks in the apartment building," Carlos said. "I bet he could have taken Mr. Gossett's camera too."

"Especially if he was mad at Mr. Gossett," Emily added.

"But what about Josh's clue?" Billy asked. "Where does that fit in?"

"Yeah, you should hear about what Josh saw," Carlos said to the girls.

Josh repeated his story about Ricky and the long-haired man in the creek bed. When he mentioned the money, his sister let out a low whistle.

"Something is going on, but what?" Emily asked. "Do you think it's a theft ring? Maybe Eddie and this long-haired man are working together. Maybe Ricky is helping them."

"Anything is possible." Josh looked carefully over at Eddie Reeser, who was cleaning up around the food tables. "Why don't we pay Eddie another visit and see if we can get him to talk?"

"Just don't get him started talking about those silly tattoos," Emily said.

"Let me see if I can get him to open up." Josh walked over toward the grill. The other Home School Detectives were right behind him.

Over by the food tables, Eddie Reeser was cleaning up around the grill. He smiled as Josh and the others walked up.

"Hi, Eddie," Josh said. "You cleaning up?"

"Spic and span, as they say." Eddie motioned toward Mr. Gossett. "It seems like someone else is trying to clean up around here too."

"Mr. Gossett is really mad about his camera being taken," Josh said.

"I'm not surprised," Eddie said. "That thing was worth a thousand bucks. At least that's what Mr. Gossett says. His insurance will pay for it since it was stolen out of his office. You don't have to worry. Mr. Gossett takes care of himself."

"At least he'll get his money back," Josh said. "He's still really mad."

"Well, he gets mad easily and blames everybody else for his problems," Eddie said. "Mr. Gossett's got a real temper. I try not to cross him. He's fired me a few times when he got mad. But he don't mean it. He always hires me back right away. He knows he couldn't get anyone else to work around here as cheaply as I do. He and the owners like cheap labor like me. They'll be sorry one day. Once I get out of school and get a real job, I'll quit this job and move out of this rat hole."

"You are in school?" Josh asked.

"You bet, over at the community college," Eddie replied. "I'm learning how to be a body man. I'm also taking basic courses in case I go on to college some day."

"What's a body man?" Emily asked.

"A person who fixes up your car when you have a wreck or want a good paint job," Eddie replied with a grin. "It's a good skill to have. People always need a good body man. I'm pretty good at it. I could make more money doing that part-time than working here. Then I could keep getting my college courses. I know a guy here in Springdale who already wants to hire me at his shop once I get done this semester. He's someone I respect and will treat me right, not like the owners of this place."

"Who are the owners?" Josh asked.

"I've never seen them," Eddie said. "They never come out here in person. They're probably ashamed to see what they've been charging people. That's one reason why Mr. Gossett was so glad he kept his precious tape from that video camera. He wants the owners to see how nice everything is when it's fixed up. Of course once they see that, they'll probably raise the rent on everyone."

"Raise the rent?" Julie asked. "They wouldn't do that."

"Nothing would surprise me about those buzzards." Eddie wiped the table with a damp rag. "They are cheap and so is Mr. Gossett. He's the biggest cheapskate of the bunch."

"Sounds like you've had some problems," Josh said carefully.

"Problems?" Eddie said. "You don't know what it's like working for him. It can be like pulling teeth to get him to pay you sometimes. And he's always got an excuse. He blames it on the renters. He says they don't pay him on time, and so he can't pay me. But that's not true. I talk to these people. If they don't pay, they don't stay. He'll put them out in the street. And

I'm the one who usually has to make them move out. Last week he had me put Mrs. Johnson and her three kids right out on the sidewalk. Everything in her whole apartment was right out there on the cement. It started to rain, but he didn't care."

"Really?" Josh asked.

"You better believe it," Eddie said. "She was crying and carrying on. Her sister finally showed up and helped pay her bill because her sister didn't want Mrs. Johnson and her kids moving in with her. So, then I had to move all Mrs. Johnson's stuff right back inside. The whole thing took three hours of my time for nothing. All I got was a sore back because he wouldn't hire someone to help me. We had just gotten everything moved back in before it really started to rain hard. But he didn't care, as long as he got his money. This is a lousy job in a lot of ways."

"Doesn't sound like much fun," Billy said.

"It isn't when you get stuck with the dirty work like kicking people out of their apartments." Eddie picked up a brush and began cleaning the grill. "I get all the complaints around here about drains that don't drain and heat that don't heat, and he just sits in his office and collects all the money. I work as fast as I can around here. But I've got a lot of schoolwork to do. I don't have time to work full-time, but he and the owners don't want to pay for another part-time maintenance man. He says they can't afford it. Meanwhile, all the people yell at me for being slow. I'm not slow. I do good work. It's just that he's cheap, the cheap buzzard."

"Why don't you just leave?" Emily asked.

"I will when I get done with school this semester and get a better job," Eddie said. "I get my rent for free here, which I need right now. But I want to move because of the roaches.

I got lots of roaches in there. I hate those buggers."

"Roaches, yuck!" Rebecca crinkled her nose.

"Well, the whole apartment building is full of them," Eddie grunted. "At least he's finally going to do something about that. Tomorrow morning we're going to kick everyone out and spray and set off bug bombs. People around here say that he's been promising to exterminate for years, but he never did. I don't know what made him so generous all of a sudden. Maybe all the nice things your church is doing is rubbing off on him, so he's more generous. He needs to spend some real money and replace the heating system."

"You don't have heat?" Josh asked with surprise.

"We've got heat, sort of." Eddie frowned. "But the furnace is ancient and dangerous, in my opinion. Of course, I live down there by it. He says the owners won't pay for it. It doesn't work right half the time. In the winter, the top-floor people are burning up and the downstairs people are freezing. The city barely passed it on the last inspection. I think Mr. Gossett might have even paid off the inspector."

"Sounds like you and he argue a lot," Josh said.

"We sure do," Eddie replied. "Two weeks ago he was in a big hurry for me to put up new smoke alarms. He went on and on about how he wanted things to be safe. So I dropped everything and installed twenty-two smoke alarms. That's a lot of smoke alarms. Of course he bought the cheapest alarms he could find, the ones without warning lights or even the little lights that tell you if your battery is good. I'm surprised he bothered at all. But the next day I found out why he was in such a big hurry. The building inspector came over and checked on the smoke alarms. Mr. Gossett doesn't care about safety. He just doesn't want to get in trouble with the inspector and get fined. Someone complained, apparently. He thinks it was me. But it wasn't. After I did all that work, up half the night, he didn't want to pay me for working overtime. I told him that he and his stupid smoke alarms could burn and go straight to . . . Well, I better not repeat myself around you kids. I just hate it when someone tries to cheat me out of money they owe me."

The muscles in Eddie's arms bulged as he cleaned the grill. Josh looked at the tattoo of the eagle. The blue-green bird looked as if it were poised to fly away.

"We were wondering if you had any ideas of who might have taken Mr. Gossett's camera," Josh said. "I think it may be the same person who took Ms. Carson's purse."

"I doubt it," Eddie said.

"Why?"

"I have my own suspicions." The maintenance man looked uneasy. "You kids don't know half the stuff that goes on around this place. But I see it all or hear about it later. You kids are lucky you live on your side of town. Things are a lot nicer over there."

"But things are getting nicer here, don't you think?" Julie asked hopefully.

"Well, they sure look nicer on the outside," Eddie said. "And I'm not saying what your church is trying to do ain't good. It really is. Everything looks a thousand percent better around here. But changing the outside don't necessarily change the inside."

"But people have worked inside the building too," Billy said. "I saw them painting in the hallways. And you said they were going to kill all the roaches tomorrow."

"I don't mean inside the apartment building. I mean in

here." Eddie tapped his chest. He looked at the fresh faces of the young people with weary eyes.

"Well, we're praying that hearts change too," Julie said.

"Hearts need to change a lot around this place, that's for sure," Eddie said.

"What makes you say that?" Josh wanted to draw Eddie out more.

"You kids are too young to understand." Eddie did not try to hide the edge in his voice. "I'll just be glad when I can get out of this place. And when I go, I'm going to tell that old buzzard Gossett what I really think of him and those cheap-skate owners. But he won't care. He'll just sit in his office counting his money, the cheap buzzard."

Josh and the others looked at Eddie as he finished cleaning up the grill. When he was done, he closed the lid. "I don't want you kids to think we're not grateful for all the help your church has been. I'm really thankful. You've made my job a lot easier. A lot of jobs are caught up now. It's just that . . . well, there's stuff that you probably don't understand."

"Well, we're praying for the people out here," Julie said quickly.

"And we'll pray for you too," Josh added.

"Thanks, I appreciate that, I really do." Eddie blinked several times. "I've been praying a little myself. I don't know if God hears prayers from a guy like me, but I'm sending a few out there."

"Of course he hears," Billy said. "God hears everything."

"Yeah, I guess so." For a moment, it looked like Eddie wanted to say more. Then he stopped. Josh and the others just looked at him. Eddie looked down at the ground as if staring at his black boots.

"Well, I need to go get my trash bags," Josh said. "I left them under the bridge."

"Under the bridge?" Eddie asked. "There's always trash down under there, that's for sure. It's a regular dump down there."

"I picked most of it up," Josh said.

"Help us put away our sacks first," Julie said. "They're really heavy. Then we'll help you with yours. Besides, we need to talk to you."

"Okay." Josh knew what Julie wanted to talk about. "We'll see you around, Eddie."

"Sure thing," Eddie said. "You kids be careful, okay?"

Josh and the others walked back over to the van. When they turned around and looked back at the barbecue grill, Eddie was gone.

"Boy, he disappeared fast," Josh said.

"I think he may be the thief," Billy said excitedly. "Did you see how guilty he looked?"

"I don't know," Julie said. "It does sound like he and Mr. Gossett don't get along."

"Yeah, and that would give him a motive for stealing Mr. Gossett's camera," Carlos said.

"Yeah, he told us he was angry at Mr. Gossett," Billy said.

"But he also said he was praying too," Julie added. "I think his heart is in the right place. I don't know if he's the thief or not."

"I didn't figure Eddie as the kind of guy who would pray either," Josh admitted.

"But what about all those things he said about Mr. Gossett?" Billy added. "He said Mr. Gossett didn't pay him for overtime work. Maybe he would steal to get the money he thinks he deserves."

"Maybe," Josh said. "But why would he steal Ms. Carson's money? He's not mad at her."

"How do you know?" Emily asked. "We don't really know much about him."

"Which means we should be careful about accusing him," Josh said. "I'm not saying he's innocent. But I think we need to investigate more."

"Let's get rid of this trash," Emily said. "We need your help to put it in the dumpster."

The boys helped the girls carry the bags of trash to the dumpster behind the apartment building. Josh and Carlos lifted the heavier bags up over into the big metal trash bin.

"Why don't you come with me and get the bags I left under the bridge." Josh said. "I may want your help in case they got dumped out again."

Josh led the way back to the broken bridge. He climbed down the creek bank on the well-worn path. He was relieved to see that no other kids were under the bridge. The two garbage bags were sitting side by side. They were both full.

"Hey, someone added trash to this other bag," Josh said. "It looks like they went up the creek beyond the bridge too."

"Yeah, it's actually clean down here," Billy said with surprise. "It used to look like a dump, like Eddie said."

"Hey, Josh, there's something here." Carlos examined the trash bags.

Josh walked over. A white piece of paper was fastened under the twist tie around the neck of the bag.

"There's writing on it." Josh undid the twist tie. "It's a note." Josh read silently. He began to frown. He looked around quickly.

"What does it say?" Billy asked impatiently.

" 'I know what's going on around here,' " Josh read from the note. " 'Meet me below the bridge tomorrow morning at eight o'clock. It's not safe to talk now. Please keep this meeting a secret.' "

Josh looked up at his friends. A gust of wind blew. The old boards in the broken bridge creaked and groaned as if they too had a secret to tell.

Chapter Six

A Good Friday?

Later that evening, Josh stood outside by the back-board in his driveway. His family had just come home from a Good Friday service at their church. Inside, everyone was getting ready for bed, but Josh felt agitated. He bounced the old ball almost mindlessly. In the distance the stars were shining. The moon was rising. He took his old, worn basketball, bounced it and caught it. He frowned at the ball.

He ran his hand over its worn surface and bit his lip. Most of the ball felt smooth to the touch since all the little bumps had been bounced away from so much use. Then Josh remembered. "Fifty-nine ninety-five plus tax," Josh said to himself. "Over sixty dollars, and I didn't even have my good ball for a full week."

Josh threw the ball down so hard that it bounced back up and bent one of his fingers as he tried to catch it. The ball careened out of his hand and shot into the garage, where it hit Emily's bicycle.

The speed of the bouncing ball was enough to tip the balance of the blue bicycle so it started to fall. Josh rushed forward hoping to stop it, but he was too late. The bike fell into a stack of cardboard boxes which tumbled over onto the wooden work bench at the back of the garage, hitting some glass baby food jars full of bolts and nuts and washers. Three of the small jars rolled off the edge of the bench to the cement floor.

The bottles broke with a popping sound, like firecrackers. Little metal nuts and bolts shot everywhere on the garage floor. Meanwhile, the basketball careened off the distant wall and ricocheted back toward Josh. The ball rolled silently up to his feet. He lifted his right toe and stopped it. He stared back at the garage, looking at the new mess his anger had caused. He sighed.

The door at the back of the garage that led into the house opened. Josh's father stood in the doorway.

"What's going on?" he asked.

"The ball got away from me and knocked over some stuff," Josh said. "I think it broke some of the baby food jars. Sorry. I'll clean it up."

His father looked at the workbench. He walked over for a closer inspection, staring at the ground.

"There's broken glass everywhere." His father didn't say it in a mean way. That was one thing Josh really liked about his dad. He didn't get mad over things like broken jars even if was the result of a stupid mistake like getting mad at a basketball.

"I'll clean it up. It's my fault." Josh bent down and picked up the basketball. He carried it into the garage and carefully set it down inside a box where it wouldn't roll away or do any more damage. Josh went to the corner and got a broom and dustpan. His father watched him.

"Rough day, huh?" his father asked.

"No kidding," Josh muttered.

"Are you still feeling bad about the purse being found in your guitar case?" his father asked.

"Yeah, some," Josh said. "But I feel worse about my basketball being stolen. I know I didn't steal Ms. Carson's purse. But I don't know who stole my basketball."

Josh bent down to sweep. He stared at all the shiny pieces of broken glass and frowned. He reached down and picked up a two-inch bolt.

"Put the nuts and bolts in the coffee can." His father had retrieved an empty coffee can from the bottom of the workbench.

Josh dropped the bolt in the can. It made a satisfying metallic clanking sound. He added another and then a washer and then a nut. For some reason he liked the way they sounded when they hit the bottom of the can.

"Be careful picking those up," his father said. "You don't want to get a sliver of glass in your finger."

"Yeah." Josh slowed down. His father was right. At that very moment he felt the prick of a piece of glass. He carefully pulled the tiny curved sliver out of his thumb and dropped it into the dustpan. He squeezed his thumb where it had been stuck. A tiny drop of red blood appeared.

"Already got one?" his father noticed.

"Yeah," Josh said with disgust. He didn't look up at his father. He picked up more bolts and nuts, dropping them into the can.

"I'm really sorry about your ball," his father said.

"Not as sorry as I am," Josh replied.

"I know I advised you not to take your ball," his dad said. "But for what it's worth, I think your heart was in the right place in taking it to the apartments and wanting to share it with the kids there."

"I wanted to share it, but not that much," Josh grunted.

"You did the right thing," Mr. Morgan said.

"But it's unfair," Josh said. "If it was the right thing, then why did my ball end up stolen? Does God want people to rip us off so we can stand around and smile about it? How is that the right thing?"

"God doesn't condone stealing, if that's what you mean," his father said.

"But if it was the right thing, how come my brand-new ball got stolen?" Josh complained. "I don't think that's fair. I was stupid for even taking my ball. I should have taken the old ball."

"Why didn't you take the old one?" his father asked.

"Because I wanted to play with my new one," Josh said. "Besides, I thought those guys out there would think it was neat that I had a really good leather ball. I thought they would like it better."

"Did they?"

"Yeah," Josh said. "They were real impressed. They were so impressed that one of them decided to keep it for himself, that's how impressed they were."

His father didn't say anything. He bent down beside his son. He started to pick up the little metal bolts and nuts, dropping them into the can too.

"I'm not trying to excuse the sins of others," his father said. "But at the same time, it's not wrong to try to give and share. In the process, things may not always turn out as you expect. It may cost you more than you figured. We've had things stolen over the years in trying to help people."

"You sound like Pastor Brown now," Josh said. "He said he had stuff stolen, even a car. Well, he said a guy borrowed it without permission and then wrecked it."

"I've heard about that car," his father said with a smile. "But I've also heard Pastor Brown say that he would have done the same thing again."

"Really?" Josh asked. "He wanted his car stolen?"

"No," his father said. "But the man who took the car and wrecked it was a drug addict. When Pastor Brown didn't press charges or even get angry, it touched the man's heart. He could tell by his actions that Pastor Brown was different from a lot of people. He could see the love of Jesus in Pastor Brown. And when he started to see Jesus, his life began to change."

"Just because of a wrecked car?" Josh asked in surprise.

"Not only that, but it was a big factor in the man's becoming a Christian," Mr. Morgan said. "That old wrecked car became a bridge for that man. A bridge to Jesus. When he saw the love of Jesus reaching to him through Pastor Brown, he was ready to change his life direction. He was able to walk across that bridge and leave his old life behind and start a new life as a Christian."

"An old car did all that?" Josh asked with skepticism.

"It wasn't really the car at all, but the love he saw in Pastor Brown," his father said. "That car wreck cost Pastor Brown something. He was insured, but since the car was old, it didn't really cover the true value to Pastor Brown. He lost money because of the car wreck. But because Pastor Brown kept a loving attitude even when it cost him personally, that man realized that Pastor Brown's love was true and real. Seeing God's love is what really changes other people's hearts."

"So you think it was all right for that drug addict to wreck Pastor Brown's only car?" Josh asked almost angrily.

"No, it was wrong to steal," his father said. "But I am saying that through that situation, God had a higher purpose, which was to show the drug addict that he was still loved in spite of all the mistakes he had made."

"It still doesn't seem right or fair." Josh threw a tiny bolt into the can. "I mean, it was Pastor Brown's car. That man didn't have any right to wreck it. It was wrong. It's wrong to steal from other people."

"Yes, it's wrong to steal," his father said. "And it's not fair when someone steals something of yours."

"It's against the law too," Josh said with disgust. "Pastor Brown told us today that Jesus said it was okay for people to take things from you and not return them. He said that people could even hit you and that you were supposed to let them hit you again if they wanted! What kind of deal is that?"

"He was talking about the Sermon on the Mount," his father said.

"Yeah, the Sermon on the Mount," Josh said. "It sounds crazy to me. Does God really expect us to do something like that? That isn't fair. In fact, it's against the law. If people steal from you, you can take them to court and put them in jail."

"That's your right under the law," his father said. "But it's also your right not to press charges and not hold it against them. Pastor Brown could have had the addict arrested and put in jail and followed the law to the letter, but he didn't. He let the man go free. When you love someone, you don't necessarily demand your legal rights. Sometimes God asks us to give up those rights in order to show his love and to serve others."

"But that's not fair," Josh protested, throwing a bolt into the coffee can. "How can God expect you to do things that aren't fair?"

"Because that's what he did himself," his father said. "What day is today?"

"Friday," Josh said.

"But what's special about this Friday? Why did we go to church tonight?"

"Oh, you mean it's Good Friday," Josh said.

"That's right," his father said. "What happened on Good Friday about two thousand years ago?"

"Jesus was killed on a cross." Josh felt like he was answering questions in Sunday school.

"Did Jesus deserve to die?" Mr. Morgan asked. "Was he guilty of any crime?"

"No."

"If he wasn't guilty of any crime, was it fair that they killed him?" his father asked.

Josh was quiet for a moment. He hadn't thought too much about the legal issues of Jesus dying on the cross. He had grown up hearing about it all his life, so he knew it happened, but he hadn't thought about it a lot. It was sort of like a package that he hadn't really examined to see what was hidden inside.

"I guess he wasn't guilty of any real crime," Josh said. "It was like a mob that killed him. They were angry at him."

"Couldn't Jesus have called angels to come help him and

rescue him from the mob?" his father asked. "Couldn't God have protected his Son?"

"Yeah, he's God, so of course he could," Josh said. "But God let him die anyway."

"Was it fair for Jesus to die like that, killed with common thieves?"

"No," Josh said softly. "I guess not."

"Was God being unfair when he let his son be murdered like that?" his father asked.

Josh didn't know what to say. He looked down at his hands. He then looked in his father's eyes. "I don't think God was being fair, really," Josh said. "I mean, Jesus didn't really have to die. God could have stopped it. Or maybe Jesus could have talked his way out of it. He could have gotten a good lawyer, maybe, if they had lawyers then. So I would say in that sense God wasn't being fair."

"Then why did God allow his own Son to be murdered by a mob of angry, ignorant people?" his father asked. "Jesus could have escaped the cross and gotten away. Why did he go through with it anyway, even though it was unfair?"

"So he could die in our place for our sins." Josh knew the right words because he had heard them all his life. But somehow, out in the garage that evening, the words didn't sound the same.

"But what motivated Jesus and God the Father to go through all that pain for us?" Mr. Morgan asked. "It wasn't fair, but he still went and died a criminal's death. Why?"

"I guess it was because he loved us," Josh said. "The Bible says God is love."

"That's right," his father said with a smile. "His love caused Jesus to die on the cross, even though it wasn't fair.

He was an innocent man, yet he suffered and died so we could be free, so we could have forgiveness for the wrong things we've done. He took our place. It wasn't an issue of fairness but of love. In the Sermon on the Mount, Jesus didn't teach people to just do the right thing, but more than that, he asks us to do the loving thing. And that's a big difference."

Josh was quiet. All the nuts and bolts had been picked up. He got the broom and began sweeping the pieces of broken glass into a pile. His father reached down with the dustpan. Josh carefully swept the glass into the pan. His father carried the pan over to the garbage can and dumped it.

"There's a little more," Josh said.

His father bent down again with the dustpan while Josh swept the last bits of glass into it. "Good job," his dad said as Josh dumped the pan.

"I guess I never thought about Jesus giving up his rights when he died," Josh said as he put away the broom.

"Sometimes we take gifts for granted because they are free to us," his dad said. "Yet they are not free to the one who gives the gift. Jesus' gift of life to us cost him his very life and a great deal of suffering along with his death."

"Yeah," Josh said. "It doesn't seem fair."

"It wasn't," his father said. "But that's what makes his love so special and great. That he loves us when we didn't love him at all. In fact he even loves those who hate him. He loved and died for the very ones who murdered him."

"That's really hard to understand," Josh said. "I guess I didn't think of it like that."

"You'll understand more as you get older," his father said, giving him a hug. "But that's what Good Friday is all about, that God so loved the world that he gave his only Son, that whoever believes in him should not perish but have eternal life."

Josh bounced his old basketball. His father ran toward the basket. Josh passed him the ball. His father shot a lay-up. The ball rolled around the rim and spun out.

"You missed!" Josh yelled. His father grabbed the ball and did a hook shot over his shoulder. This time the ball sailed through the air and dropped through the basket without touching the rim. The net whispered as the ball passed through.

"Swish!" his father yelled. "Two points."

Josh ran for the ball. He picked it up and began to dribble. His father rushed in to guard. Josh turned and tried a hook, but his father blocked it and caught the ball. He dribbled away from the basket, and then with one smooth motion he flipped the ball around his back and passed the ball to Josh. Josh leaped up and shot. The ball bounced off the backboard and into the net.

"Two points!" his father yelled, running forward to catch the ball before it hit the ground.

"Good pass," Josh said in admiration. His father had played on the university basketball team many years before and still hadn't lost his touch.

"Good lay-up." His father held the ball in his hands and looked at it. He ran his hands over the smooth surface.

"See how worn out that ball is?" Josh asked. "You can even see the black rubber in a few places."

"She's about had it, that's for sure." His father flipped the ball up and spun it on his finger. The ball twirled rapidly. Josh marveled that his father could have such balance.

"How do you do that?" Josh asked.

"Lots of practice and patience when I had lots of spare

time," his father said. "You know you're not busy when you can learn to spin a basketball on the tip of your finger. That's one of the luxuries of youth, hanging around the basketball court with friends, talking, and spinning a basketball on your finger until you learn to make it stay."

His father watched the ball slow down and roll off the side of his finger. He caught the ball and tossed it to Josh.

"You did the right thing in taking your good ball today," his father said. "When we give, God always asks us to give our best. And that's what you did."

"He sure took it too." Josh looked at his old ball. Somehow he didn't miss the new ball as much. After talking with his father, he felt better, even though his new basketball was just as gone as before. Josh wasn't sure what happened to all those bitter feelings, but it was a relief to lose them. Being angry and bitter was no fun. Part of him wanted to hang on to the bitterness, but another part seemed to want to let go and laugh. Josh didn't understand how his feelings could change, or how he could feel two different things at once.

"Even though you lost your basketball, got falsely accused of stealing, and worked really hard, it's been a good Friday," his father said. "What do you think?"

"I don't know." In that moment Josh could see the tear-streaked face of Ms. Carson as she wailed about her lost money. "I guess it was good in some ways and bad in others. I sure hope we can catch the thief."

"You still feel like others suspect you?"

"Yes, but it's not just that I want my name cleared, or my basketball back," Josh said. "I guess I do want those things. I wish things were different over at Bridgewood. I feel sorry for a lot of those people."

"Well, you helped make a difference today, and that's a start," his father said. "It's late. We'd better go to bed now."

Josh nodded. Later, in bed, he looked up in the darkness. He thought about Jesus being murdered. He tried to imagine the scene. He had watched it in movies and videos, but he wondered what it was really like on that Friday so many years ago.

"How could he let them?" Josh fell asleep asking questions that only led to more questions. He fell asleep wondering if life would always be like that.

Chapter Seven

The Meeting at Eight

Josh woke up with the sunlight streaming through his window. He had slept longer than he expected. His family had already eaten breakfast. Josh felt too rushed to stop and eat. He found Emily in the garage, working on her bicycle.

"Someone knocked my bike over, and it messed up the hand brake," Emily said. "I bet it was Robby. He said he didn't, but I think he was lying."

"Actually, it was me," Josh said. "I accidentally hit it with the basketball last night."

"Well, you messed up my brake handle," Emily said flatly. Her mouth curled as she tightened the wrench.

"Don't pull it too tight or you'll strip it," Josh warned.

"Then you do it." Emily handed him the wrench. "You messed it up."

Josh bent down and began working on the brake. When he

was done, he began working on the other brake. He kept tinkering, going back and forth, squeezing the brakes until they were right.

"There, they're both adjusted," Josh said with satisfaction. "Now let's go out to Bridgewood. Whoever wrote that note wants to meet at eight o'clock sharp."

"Do you think that's a real clue?" Emily asked suspiciously. "What if that note wasn't even for us? Why are they being so secretive?"

"I don't know," Josh replied as he swung his leg over his bike frame. He pulled on his bike helmet and tightened the strap under his chin. "It's the only clue we have to go on at this point. Billy and Carlos want to check it out."

"You guys go ahead," Emily replied. "I don't want to be around there when they kill all the cockroaches. Rebecca says when they fumigate a building that all the roaches run outside to get away. I don't want them crawling on me. That would be a nightmare."

"They don't really do that," Josh said in disbelief.

"That's what Rebecca said," Emily replied firmly. "I believe her. Besides, I'm going over to see Julie. We might go over there later, just to see what you found out. But if I see roaches running around on the ground, I'm not even going to slow down."

"Okay, you big chicken." Josh laughed as he pushed his bike out into the street and began pedaling toward Carlos's house. Billy and Carlos were already waiting in the street.

"We'll be late if we don't hurry," Carlos said.

"Let's go then." Josh took the lead. The Saturday morning air felt fresh and cool on his face. The day seemed wide open before him, and that felt good. Soon they were all cruising through the middle of Springdale, heading to the other side of town.

As they turned onto Blanchard Street, Josh saw the flashing red lights at the far end of the street. A police car was parked in the street in front of the Bridgewood Apartments.

"Let's go!" Josh yelled at the others. He pedaled faster. Carlos and Billy hurried to catch up. Josh angled off the road as he rode beyond the police car because a canvas fire hose was stretched across the street.

Josh followed the hose through the parking lot to the side of the apartments. A big red fire engine was parked near the creek. Men in long black-and-yellow fire coats were busy working around the truck. Josh slowed down suddenly. Billy had to swerve to avoid running into the rear of Josh's bike.

"Don't stop like that!" Billy yelled as he jerked his handlebars again to miss hitting a tree trunk.

"It's the old broken bridge." Carlos came to a stop. The boys parked their bikes away from any flow of traffic. Then they all ran toward the creek. Lots of people were standing on both sides of the creek, looking at the smoldering ruins of the bridge. All that was left were a few smoking boards lying in the bottom of the creek bed. The old metal sign with the blue cross was lying on top. Though it was sooty, the cross was still very visible, and Jesus' name was still printed with a backward *S*.

"Burned to the ground," Billy whispered.

"You can say that again," Carlos added.

Josh looked at the crowds of people standing on the creek banks. On the Bridgewood side were many of the faces from yesterday. Some of the older people in the apartments had worn their bathrobes and slippers outside. Chester and others stood in a group farther away. Josh looked for Ricky but didn't see him among the others. Josh recognized Mike and Antonio from the Gateway Apartments standing across the creek. The rest were just strangers.

"What about our meeting?" Billy asked. "We were supposed to meet whoever wrote that note under the bridge."

"Now there's no bridge to meet under," Carlos said.

"I was thinking the same thing," Josh said. "And we don't even know who we're trying to meet."

"I don't think they'll talk to us with all these people standing around," Billy observed.

"Yeah, it looks like we're out of luck on our last clue," Carlos added.

"Maybe." Josh scanned the faces in the crowd near the fire truck, hoping someone would try to catch his eye. But no one even seemed to notice Josh and the other two boys. Josh looked back at the burned-out bridge with a frown.

"What a waste." Josh looked at the smoldering embers.

"Well, it was falling down anyway," Billy said.

"Somebody must have set it on fire," Josh said. "That bridge didn't burn down by itself."

"I wonder who did it," Carlos said.

"The bridge kids, of course," Billy replied. "One of them had to set it. I bet it was the Gateway kids."

"Why them?" Josh asked.

"Because the bridge is really closer to the Bridgewood Apartments," Billy said. "I think the Gateway kids are jealous and wanted to destroy it."

"But kids on both sides of the creek hung out here," Carlos said. "I think it was the Bridgewood kids. They hung out under here more, I bet. Besides, they were the ones who set the trash on fire in the dumpster a few weeks ago."

"They were suspected of setting that fire, but they denied it," Josh said.

"Mr. Gossett seemed to think they set it," Carlos replied.

"I don't think any of the bridge kids would burn down the bridge," Josh said.

"Why not?" Billy asked.

"Because it was their hangout," Josh replied. "Now they don't have a place to go. Both sides claimed it. I just don't think they would burn it down."

"But they could have done it unintentionally," Carlos said. "They could have been smoking or playing with matches and gotten careless."

"Maybe." Josh frowned as he looked at the smoldering boards. He scanned the crowd of faces again. Then he looked across the creek at the people lined up over there. Some were already walking away.

Over by the fire truck, Mr. Gossett was talking to the firefighters, who were rolling up the hoses. Mr. Gossett's face was red, and he looked upset. Josh walked closer.

" . . . and I want this person caught and caught today," Mr. Gossett was saying. "That's two fires in two weeks, and that's two fires too many."

"We'll do the best we can, Mr. Gossett," the firefighter responded patiently.

"Sounds like we have another mystery to solve here," Billy whispered to Josh.

"I want this arsonist caught," Mr. Gossett said, as if he had not heard the firefighter speak. "I want him caught, and I want him caught yesterday."

"You need to talk to the police about that." The firefighter finished winding up a hose.

"You can be sure that I will." The big man turned and walked briskly away.

"He's hotter than a firecracker, ain't he?" a voice asked. Josh turned around quickly.

Eddie Reeser's face was covered with black sooty smudges. His white undershirt was worse. His arms were wet with sweat. His blue jeans were covered with soot and his boots were muddy.

"What happened to you?" Billy asked with wide eyes. "You're a mess."

"I was the first one at the scene." Eddie pulled a crumpled pack of cigarettes out of his hip pocket. He pulled a bent cigarette out and looked at it in disgust. He straightened the cigarette, put it in his mouth, lit it with a blue disposable lighter, took a deep puff and blew the smoke out.

"It looks like someone tried to set you on fire," Josh said.

"I was out here with the garden hose and got too close," Eddie said, nodding his head. "You'd think I wouldn't want to smoke after breathing a bunch of smoke already this morning. It's a bad habit. Don't you kids ever start to smoke, okay?"

"We won't." Billy crinkled his nose at the smell of the smoke.

"Good, because it's really bad for you," Eddie said. "I should stop. I'm going to stop once I get my new job and start working in the shop. I am going to stop for sure."

"How do you think the fire got started?" Josh asked. "Do you think the kids were smoking down there and got careless?"

"They do smoke down there," Eddie said. "But that didn't

start that fire. It was set. The whole thing went up like *that* at four o'clock this morning." Eddie snapped his fingers.

"You think it was arson?" Josh asked.

"I know it was arson," Eddie replied. "Nothing would make that bridge burn like that unless it was arson. I was the first person down there. Mrs. Johnson saw it from her window. She came down and woke me up, pounding on my door. Her dog was barking and barking. It was already burning hard by the time I got dressed. I got the hose and ran over, but it was too far gone. I could smell the gasoline, though."

"Gas?" Josh asked.

"Yeah, I even found a can down in the creek bed," Eddie replied. "The firefighters had it, though they may have given it to the police by now. It was the gas can we keep in our utility shed here for the lawnmower."

"You mean someone put gas on the bridge and set it on fire on purpose?" Billy asked.

"That gas can didn't walk over there by itself," Eddie replied. "Besides, it had to be gas to be burning that fast. That bridge was in flames. Someone doused it good and set it burning. Mr. Gossett got here about as quick as the fire engines. He thinks someone around here did it. He's been yelling at everyone saying they should have put it out. But no one could have put that fire out. He's got no right yelling at everyone this early on a Saturday morning. The firefighters did their job, and I was doing my job. The old bridge was falling apart anyway."

Several people from the apartment were outside standing around, watching the firefighters and police. Ms. Carson, who was dressed in a bathrobe, was talking to Deputy Haskins. Her hair was covered with a scarf. She looked miserable.

"Ms. Carson still looks upset over losing her money," Josh said.

"That's not it," Eddie said.

"What do you mean?" Josh asked.

"Her kid is gone." Eddie took another deep puff on the cigarette and dropped it on the ground, stepping on it. "She woke up this morning when the fire trucks came, and Ricky was gone. She said he went out last night and didn't ever come home. She's plenty worried."

"He ran away from home?" Billy asked.

"Sounds like it," Eddie said. "Of course, he could be lying in a ditch somewhere dead for all she'd know or care. She don't look after him. She's gone at night more than Ricky. She goes out all the time. She's got more problems than her own kid."

"How do you know that?" Josh asked curiously.

"Look, when you're the maintenance man, you either see things or hear it from the other renters," Eddie said. "The old folks will fill your ears with that stuff. Me, I don't really ask to hear gossip, but people will tell it to you whether you want to hear it or not. Everyone knows about Judy's problems around here."

"What problems?" Josh asked.

Eddie looked at Josh quietly. He then took a deep breath and sighed.

"I don't want to be gossiping," Eddie said finally. He pulled another cigarette out of the crumpled pack. "Plus it's none of my business, the stuff that goes on around here, since I plan to be leaving. But I'll tell you this: I'm not surprised Ricky Carson is gone. I'd probably take off too if I was that kid, the way his mom acts."

"You think it was good for him to run away?" Billy asked.

"I didn't say that," Eddie said quickly. He lit his cigarette. "I'm just saying I'm not surprised. I felt sorry for the kid. I've had to help him get his mother inside their apartment more than once because she was so out of it."

"Help her how?" Carlos asked.

"Help her walk," Eddie said. "The poor kid would come home and find her passed out in the hall, and he can't move her. He'd be ashamed to let his friends see her like that, though they know all about it. So I'd help him get her inside and lay her on the couch and let her sleep it off."

"She was drunk?"

"Drunk or high, what difference does it make to a twelve-year-old kid when his mom is lying out in the hall?" Eddie said. "I feel sorry for the kid. Of course she won't tell the police that's why he ran off. She's a woman who can't face her problems. I've talked to her, told her she needs to get help, but she always has an excuse. You can't help people like that when they don't want help. Believe me, I know. My oldest brother was like that."

"Did he have a drinking problem?" Josh asked.

"Drinking and drugs," Eddie said. "I hardly knew him because he's fifteen years older than me. I'm the baby in our family. But Frank, my oldest brother, finally got straightened out. He almost died before he started facing his problems. But now he's got a good job and a family. He lives in Dallas. Your father knows him."

"My dad?" Carlos asked.

"He sure does," Eddie said. "A long time ago Frank used to live around here. He borrowed your dad's old car one time, and he went out and wrecked it. Almost killed himself.

Totaled the car. But your dad was real good about it. He could have had Frank thrown in jail for a long time. But instead, he kept trying to help him. Frank got his life turned around after that. Now he goes to church and is living a good clean life. He's a manager of a furniture store."

"I've heard about that car," Carlos said.

"Me too," Josh added. "That was your brother?"

"Yeah, sure was," Eddie said. "I was just a little kid way back then, younger than you guys even. But I know Frank's been grateful ever since. He was going downhill fast. He probably would have been in jail or dead by now if he hadn't known your dad. Whenever I see him, he tells me how God turned his life around."

"Pastor Brown never said it was your brother," Josh said.

"That's because he doesn't gossip like the people around this place," Eddie said. "I respect that in a person. Look, I probably said too much about Judy as it is. I just feel sorry for Ricky, that's all. But I don't trust Judy. Just between you and me, I was a little surprised to hear your church gave her three hundred dollars yesterday."

"They did?" Josh asked.

"They sure did," Eddie replied. "Didn't they tell you? I guess they felt sorry that her purse got stolen and took up a collection or something. I heard her talking about getting the money. I hope she paid her rent right away and doesn't go out and spend it on booze or something like that. I'm sure ol' man Gossett had his hand out the minute she got that money. But you never know. He and Judy have been real friendly with one another lately. He seemed awful generous yesterday, saying that he could work out a deal with her rent money being gone. He's not usually like that with any of the other renters. He puts them on the street if they can't pay up. Of course he might have just been doing that so he would look like a big generous guy in front of everyone, which he is not. He's a totally cheap buzzard."

"You really don't like Mr. Gossett very much, do you?" Josh asked.

"Not hardly." Eddie wiped his muddy boot on the grass. "And for good reasons. I don't like him, and I don't trust him. I need to get cleaned up. You kids take care now."

Eddie Reeser turned and walked toward the apartment building. He opened the door at the end of the hallway and disappeared inside.

"Eddie isn't shy about telling you how he feels, is he?" Josh asked.

"Nope," Carlos said. "I would have never known that was his brother who took my father's car. That was before any of us were even born."

"He sure is a funny guy," Billy said. "Yesterday I was sure he was the one who took Ms. Carson's money and maybe Mr. Gossett's camera. But today I'm not sure what to think."

"Me either," Josh said. "I wish we could have met whoever wrote the note."

Josh walked over to the creek bank near the burned bridge. He stared down at the smoking embers. He followed the path down into the creek bed. He looked over toward where the bridge had been. Two huge concrete footing blocks stood charred and blackened on either side of the creek bank. The bridge had rested on the two heavy blocks. They looked exposed and ugly in the morning light. Josh wandered closer, being careful to step on larger rocks so his feet could avoid all the mud from the fire hoses. He bent down and carefully touched the burnt metal sign. His finger traced the outline of the smoky blue cross.

"I got a message for you," a voice said. Josh looked up. Chester Jones stood alone on the cement footing on the Bridgewood side.

"What?" Josh asked.

"I said I got a message for you," Chester said. "Come up here. I'm not going to shout it."

Josh nodded and scrambled up the creek bank. When he got to the top, he motioned for Billy and Carlos to come over. The three boys gathered around Chester, who looked uneasy.

"Are you the one who left the note?" Josh asked.

"I don't know anything about a note," Chester said. "But I got a friend who said you'd be down by the bridge this morning. He told me to tell you to meet him out of town on Drew Road toward Centerville. Go out about a mile or so, and you'll find him or he'll find you. Do you know where Drew Road is?"

"Sure, it's right down the block from here," Josh said.

"That's the one," Chester said. "And he said meet him right away, as soon as possible. He said he'll be waiting. Just keep going until you find him."

"Who is it?" Josh asked.

"He doesn't want me to say." Chester looked at his feet.

"Why won't you tell us?" Billy asked.

"I'm telling you all you need to know." The tall boy turned and walked quickly away.

Chapter Eight

Drew Road

This is really getting weird," Billy said as they got on their bicycles.

"I know," Josh said. "But Drew Road isn't far away. It's just down the block. We can pedal out there without too much trouble."

The boys jumped on their bikes and headed across the lawn. They passed Mr. Gossett in the parking lot. He and Ms. Carson were still talking to the police officer, who was busily writing on a clipboard. They pedaled through the parking lot.

They saw Chester walk quickly in front of them and around the corner of the apartment building. He looked unhappy when he saw Josh. The tall young man looked down at the ground, avoiding Josh's eyes, and walked through the front door of the building.

"What's the matter with him?" Billy asked, noticing Chester's behavior.

"Who knows?" Just then Josh saw a man with long brown hair standing at the end of the apartment building, peeking around the corner. Josh almost hit his brakes. He kept going but pedaled slower.

"I just saw that man who gave money to Ricky yesterday," Josh whispered to Billy and Carlos. He pedaled to the end of the parking lot and stopped behind a car. The others stopped.

"Where?" Billy asked. Josh pointed to the corner of the apartment building.

"He's acting kind of sneaky," Carlos said. "Chester was right there. Do you think he and Chester were talking?"

"They must have seen each other at least," Josh said. "But who is that guy?"

"Look, he's running away," Billy said. The man with long hair ran along the side of the apartment building and disappeared around the corner.

"Look, here comes Mr. Gossett and Ricky's mom," Carlos said. The three boys watched the big man and short lady hurry across the parking lot.

"They must have seen him," Josh said. "Something sure spooked him. Yesterday I heard him say he didn't want to be seen around here."

The couple hurried around the corner of the building. Before long they were out of sight.

"What's going on around here?" Carlos wondered.

"Beats me," Josh said. "The more you see and hear, the more you don't understand. I say we go out to Drew Road and find whoever wrote that note. Let's go."

Josh pushed down on his pedals to speed up. Drew Road was only a block away.

"This is it," Josh cried out as he turned onto the road. He

changed gears, and the bike started moving faster. Drew Road was deserted. It led out quickly into the country. Josh took deep breaths as he kept up his fast pace. The other boys followed from behind, astonished at Josh's energy.

"It's not a race, is it?" Billy asked, beginning to pant as they crossed over a set of railroad tracks. "I don't know if I can keep up with him."

"He's going like a wild man," Carlos panted. He was beginning to sweat and wiped his face with his arm. "I don't know why he's in such a hurry. Hey, Josh! Slow down!"

Josh heard the cries of his friends behind him. He stopped pedaling and coasted. He was surprised to see that Billy and Carlos were already thirty yards behind him.

"Hurry up!" he yelled back at his friends.

"Wait up!" Billy yelled back. "You're going too fast."

Josh let his bike coast to a stop. He put his foot down on the pavement and looked down the road to see if he could see the one who made the mystery appointment. The road looked clear as far as he could see. But it curved behind some trees about a quarter of a mile away. Josh looked back at his friends. They were panting as they rode up to him.

"What's . . . your . . . hurry?" Carlos gasped out. "You're going like that thing is a motorcycle."

"Yeah," Billy said. "Where'd you learn to ride so fast?"

"I just don't want to miss meeting whoever wrote that note," Josh said. "Chester said we needed to hurry. Besides, I've got a feeling, like something bad is going to happen."

"Don't get so far ahead," Billy protested.

"We shouldn't ride side by side on a narrow road like this one," Josh said.

"I don't care about riding side by side. I just want us to

stick together," Billy said. "You'll be in the next county if you don't wait for us."

"I'll slow down, but I want you guys to speed up," Josh said.

"Okay," Billy said with grim determination. Carlos didn't say a word. He was saving his energy. All three boys sped along the road as it led out into the country. On the right was a string of telephone poles and wires. Plowed fields waiting for seeds bordered both sides of the country road. The fields stopped at a stand of trees where the road curved.

Josh sped up as he reached the curve, driven by his curiosity. He wanted to see what was on the other side of the curve. He didn't know what to expect. The boys kept pedaling. Birds and moving branches caught Josh's eye, so he pedaled slower. Each time he saw something move, he thought it might be the mystery person who sent the note.

Josh pedaled along, glad to be in the shade of the trees. The shadowy road was very quiet. The loudest sound was the bicycle tires on the pavement. The road curved again and the forest ended, opening up in another section of flat fields. In the distance, far on the horizon, a farmer was guiding a green tractor out in the field. A faint chugging noise could be heard. Josh slowed down to a stop. "We've come a mile at least." He looked at his watch. "I don't see anyone, though."

"Did Chester say to come a mile exactly, or about a mile?" Billy asked.

"He said to go about a mile," Carlos replied. "But I don't see anyone."

"Do you think he was telling us the truth?" Carlos asked. "Maybe he was just sending us on some wild goose chase."

"Why would he do that?" Josh asked. "He knew that we

were trying to meet someone under the bridge. I think he was telling the truth."

Buzzards were circling high overhead in the blue sky down the road away from town. Josh looked up at them and pointed.

"They give me the creeps," Josh said.

"Me too," Billy added as he looked. "When I see buzzards flying around like that, I wonder if someone is lying on the ground somewhere about to die."

"I think that sometimes too," Josh said.

"You guys have seen too much television," Carlos said, mocking.

"Well, it's probably just a dead possum," Josh said with a crooked grin. He looked up. "They are circling further down the road. I say we go further."

"I think we should just turn around and go back to town," Carlos groaned. "I don't see anyone anywhere. This is a waste of time."

"But the road curves again beyond those trees down there." Josh pointed ahead of them.

"That's more than half a mile away," Carlos groaned.

"Well, sometimes you go the second mile," Josh said seriously. He pushed off with his foot and began pedaling. Mindful of his friends' lack of enthusiasm, Josh pedaled slower this time. He shouted back encouragement. "Let's just go to those trees, and if we don't see anyone, we'll turn back. Parker Road intersects with Drew Road somewhere down there. We can take it back to Springdale if you want."

"Yeah, it goes to our side of town," Carlos said. "We can go home and watch television or do something fun."

Billy followed Josh. Carlos groaned, but he began to pedal after his two friends. The three boys pedaled with determination. Josh couldn't help but look up at the buzzards flying overhead. The farther down the road they went, the closer they got to the buzzards.

Josh secretly wondered if Carlos was right. Maybe it was just a wild goose chase. None of them knew Chester that well or the mystery person who had written the note. He didn't blame Carlos for being skeptical.

Finally they reached the trees where the road began to curve again. Josh was glad to be in the cool morning shade.

"I know what it is!" Billy said suddenly and loudly. "I know what's been bothering me. Stop your bikes!"

"What are you yelling about?" Josh said as he turned his bike around in the road, circling back to Billy and Carlos.

"I know what's been bothering me," Billy said excitedly. "I've been thinking about it since yesterday."

"Thinking about what?"

"The batteries," Billy said.

"Batteries?" Josh asked. "What in the world are you talking about? You are making no sense whatsoever."

"I'm trying to tell you," Billy said, getting more and more excited. His eyes were bright, and he looked at his two friends as if they should be able to see it too. "You know how you think of something, yet you can't quite put your finger on it, so it keeps bothering you and bothering you?"

"I guess," Carlos said doubtfully.

"Well, ever since yesterday something's been bothering me, and I couldn't figure out what it was, even though I tried," Billy said. "But I finally just thought of it."

"And it has something to do with batteries?" Josh asked.

"That's right," Billy said. "When we talked with Eddie Reeser, he said something about the smoke alarms. He said that Mr. Gossett had him put up new smoke alarms in the apartment building recently."

"Yeah, he was angry because he made him work over-time," Josh said.

"And because Mr. Gossett got the cheaper alarms," Carlos added.

"That's right," Billy said. "But yesterday after lunch, I was walking in the hallway and saw Mr. Gossett changing the battery in the smoke alarm near the recreation room. I was carrying my sack of trash. I cut through the apartments because it was shorter."

"So what?" Josh asked.

"Well, Mr. Gossett had a handful of batteries, and he dumped them in the trash can in the recreation room," Billy said. "They were the nine-volt kind, which you can use on the radio control for remote-control cars."

"I still don't get the point," Carlos said.

"Well, after he left, I stopped and got the nine-volt batteries out of the trash," Billy said. "There were six of them. I tested one to see if it still had some juice in it."

"How did you test it?" Josh asked.

"You know, by touching both terminals on your tongue," Billy said. "A good battery will give you a shock."

"That's right." Carlos grinned. "Of course it's wiser to use a battery tester."

"I only tested one with my tongue because it really shocked me," Billy said. "It really hurt my tongue. And last night, when I got home, I used my dad's battery tester, and all the other batteries were good. In fact they tested like new."

"So what's the point, Billy?" Josh asked.

"Well, I figured I just got lucky, getting six really good

batteries like that," Billy said. "But something bothered me about it. And it finally hit me. Eddie Reeser kept saying over and over that Mr. Gossett is a cheap buzzard. I was looking up at those buzzards in the sky, and it hit me. If he's so cheap, why did he throw out good batteries?"

"That's your big point?" Josh asked, not trying to hide the irritation in his voice. "He probably just wants to be safe, that's all."

"But Eddie told us he just put those smoke alarms in recently," Billy said. "Mr. Gossett knew they were new. He must have given Eddie the batteries to put in there. He must have known they were new."

"That's right," Carlos said. "I see what you mean. It is kind of odd. If he's as cheap as Eddie says, he probably wouldn't throw out good batteries. My grandfather is like that. He's so cheap that he keeps everything. His house is full of junk. My grandmother hates it, but he won't let her throw stuff away."

"I don't see what the big mystery is," Josh replied with a frown. "Mr. Gossett was just trying to be safe, that's all. Since everybody was fixing things up, he was probably just being extra careful."

"But the thing is, he looked at me funny when he saw me looking at him," Billy said. "I mean, I was just carrying a bag of trash down the hallway. But he looked at me like he didn't want me there. It seemed suspicious."

"Maybe he thought you would spill trash in the hallway," Josh said with a grin. "I don't blame him."

"I didn't spill anything!" Billy said defiantly. "I'm telling you, it was a suspicious look."

"Okay, it was suspicious, but what does it prove?" Josh asked.

"I don't know for sure," Billy said defensively. "It was just bothering me. You have to go on hunches, you know, in the detective business. You said you had a feeling and that that's why we're on this wild goose chase, cause of your bad feeling. Why can't I have a hunch?"

Josh smiled. He looked up. The buzzards still circled high in the air ahead of them. He had just begun to pedal when a loud crack split the air.

"That sounded like a gunshot!" Josh said, hitting the brakes.

"Or a firecracker," Billy added.

"Maybe it was a backfire," Carlos said. "But where did it come from?"

"Up ahead, I think." Josh looked behind them. As far as he could see, the road was empty. "Let's keep going." Josh looked at his friends with concern. He hadn't planned on hearing gunshots on this excursion. For a moment, he wondered if they should turn back. But curiosity drove him on.

"It might just be hunters," Josh said quietly.

"But it's not hunting season," Carlos said. "Not in spring. It could be someone practicing with a gun."

"Maybe, but I don't want any bullets flying around me," Billy said. "Maybe we should turn back."

Another loud crack split the air. All three boys hit the brakes automatically.

"Up there," Josh whispered. He jumped off his bike and pushed it to the left side of the road, all the way into the trees. The other boys followed him.

"What's going on?" Carlos looked where Josh was staring. Far down the road, just about where the trees cleared, a black car and a blue car were parked on the side of the road. Two men and a boy were on the shoulder of the road. One of the men was holding something that looked like a gun, and it looked like he was pointing it straight at the other man's chest.

Chapter Nine

What the Boys Saw

Do you think they saw us?" Billy asked.

"I don't know." Josh was breathing hard. He looked out from behind the tree as far down the road as he could see. "But that big man looks sort of like Mr. Gossett. And that boy looks like Ricky."

"I think we've come far enough." Billy looked at the others. He didn't try to hide his fear.

"Maybe we can get closer without being seen." Josh turned and walked deeper into the forest.

"Josh, wait up!" Carlos whispered. "What are you doing?"

He grabbed Josh by the arm and held on. Josh whirled around.

"What's wrong?" Josh asked.

"We can't just go up there," Carlos said. "What if they see us?"

"They won't see us if we stay in the forest," Josh said.

"Maybe we should go back to town," Carlos replied.

"It will take too long," Josh said. "Besides, if that's Mr. Gossett, and he's going back to Springdale on Drew Road, he'll recognize us."

"How did they get out there?" Carlos asked. "No one passed us."

"He must have come out on Parker Road from town," Josh said.

"It's like we're trapped." Billy's eyes were wide.

"We aren't trapped if they don't see us." Josh began walking through the forest. Carlos and Billy walked quickly after him.

"What about our bikes?" Billy asked.

"No one can see them from the road. They'll be okay," Josh said. Seeing the concern on his two friends' faces made him stop. "Look, we can go deeper into the woods and circle back out when we get near the cars. They won't see us if we're careful."

"Are you sure?" Carlos asked.

"Pretty sure," Josh said. "Look, let's just try it. If someone sees us, we can always run away, can't we?"

"You can't outrun a bullet," Billy said doubtfully.

"No one is going to shoot at us because they won't see us," Josh insisted. "Now let's go so we can see what's going on. It might not be Mr. Gossett. It may just be hunters or something."

"What if they want to come hunting in the woods where we are?" Billy asked.

"We'll shout out and tell them not to shoot," Josh said.

"What if it's not hunters?" Carlos asked.

"That's what I want to find out," Josh said. "Let's go."

Josh led the way. Carlos and Billy were right behind him. The woods didn't have much undergrowth, so walking was easy. But Josh still felt exposed. He moved away from the road for several yards and then stopped.

"Let's go parallel to the road now," Josh whispered to the others. They nodded.

Josh walked carefully in between the trees. The forest floor was covered with old leaves, but they were soft from decay over the winter so the boys' feet barely made a sound.

The boys walked single file for almost fifty yards. All the while, Josh kept looking to their right to make sure they wouldn't be seen. They came upon an old dirt road in the woods that looked like it hadn't been used in a long time.

"Let's follow this back toward Drew Road," Josh whispered finally. He could feel his heart beating more loudly in his chest as he crept along. He bent down lower to the ground. He kept his eyes trained ahead of him, watching for the two men. Up ahead, the trees were thinning and Josh could see the clearing and the shoulder of the road.

Then he saw the black roof of one car. Josh crouched down. He moved off the dirt road back among the trees. He began to crawl. He motioned for Billy and the others to follow. On ground level, Josh felt safer. Up ahead, a large fallen tree trunk and line of brush hid them from view. He crawled all the way to the tree trunk and stopped and waited for Billy and Carlos to join him. He slowly raised his head. He could hear angry voices.

At first he could see only one person, but he recognized him right away. It was the long-haired man. At that moment, the long-haired man pulled away, but it was too late. Josh saw the butt of a rifle hit him on the side of the head. Mr. Gossett stepped forward into view and looked down, his red face glaring.

"Dad!" a voice yelled out in horror. Ricky Carson came into view. He bent down to look at the fallen man. Josh raised his head higher to get a better look. A line of blood appeared on the cheek of the long-haired man. Mr. Gossett smiled contemptuously. He kicked the man in the side.

"Stop it!" Ricky yelled. "I won't say anything!"

"You sure won't," Mr. Gossett said. "Neither of you. I'm going to be sure of that."

The big man pulled something shiny out of his pocket. He threw it down at Ricky's feet. They were shiny, chrome handcuffs.

"Put his hands behind his back and strap those on!" The big man pointed the gun at Ricky.

"I'll do it. I'll do it." Ricky's hands shook as he picked up the handcuffs. He pulled his father's arms around to his back. He attached one cuff to each wrist. His father groaned into the dirt.

"Get up!" Mr. Gossett grunted and turned to the trunk of the old blue Oldsmobile. He searched the key ring and tried a key. He tried another, and the big trunk popped open.

"What are you going to do?" Ricky asked fearfully.

"I'm not going to do a thing." The big man smiled. "You are going to get your father into the trunk."

"But he's hurt, and he——"

"Do it now!" the big man ordered. His big face turned reddish purple in anger. "You're the one who had to stick your nose into my business. Now quit stalling and get him in there."

"But he's hurt!"

Mr. Gossett pulled back his foot and swung it forward. The

man on the ground moaned as the shoe cracked his ribs.

"In the trunk, now!" Mr. Gossett said.

Ricky pulled on his father's arms. The long-haired man sat up, shaking his head as if in a haze of groggy pain.

"You need to get in the trunk," Ricky whispered fearfully. "Please, Dad, just do what he says."

The long-haired man groaned and his eyes rolled. He didn't seem to understand exactly what the boy was saying. He did rise up to a half crouch. Ricky guided him the few steps to the open trunk of the blue car. His father slumped forward over the bumper.

"That's right, all the way in," Mr. Gossett said.

Ricky pushed his father even farther forward, tipping him all the way in. Ricky grabbed his feet and lifted his legs, straining under their weight. He lunged forward until the legs dropped into the trunk as well. His father moaned again, his face pressed against the spare tire.

"Now you," Mr. Gossett said.

"Me?"

"That's right, in the trunk," he said.

"But we'll suffocate if you close us in."

"You won't suffocate," the big man said. "This old rat trap is full of holes. Now climb in."

Ricky examined the trunk for a free space. He gingerly climbed in, trying not to step on his father.

"Lie down," Mr. Gossett said impatiently.

The boy did as he was told. Mr. Gossett slammed the trunk down quickly. The big man looked up and down the highway cautiously.

"You two be good," Mr. Gossett said. "I'll be back later."

He walked quickly around to the driver's side of the car,

opened the door and sat down. He found the right key and started the car. He pulled it slowly off the road onto the dirt road that led through the forest. He pulled thirty yards into the woods and then turned off the engine.

Josh and the others raised their heads to watch. The big man got out. He slammed the door and pocketed the keys.

"Don't go anywhere!" the big man said to the trunk. He laughed, turned away and walked quickly back to the paved road. He got into his new black car and started it. His tires spun gravel and dirt as he pulled back onto the road. He sped up and disappeared down Drew Road.

Chapter Ten

The Setup

Quick!" Josh ran toward the blue car. Billy and Carlos were right behind him. Josh reached out and tapped gently on the trunk.

"Ricky, are you all right?" Josh yelled.

"Help me!" Ricky's muffled voice shouted.

"Ricky, it's me, Josh Morgan."

"Mr. Gossett put us in here," Ricky shouted. "Get us out."

"We'll try, but I don't see how we can do it," Josh said. "The trunk is locked. He took the keys with him."

"Then you've got to get to town!" Ricky shouted. "Eddie's in danger. They're going to set him up. I heard them talking. You have to hurry before it's too late."

"Who's going to set him up?" Carlos asked.

"Mr. Gossett and my mom," Ricky said. "Please hurry. Find Eddie. Tell him what's going on. Get the police."

"I don't understand," Josh said.

"Just go get Eddie," Ricky shouted. "And tell the police. They're going to set Eddie up for the fire and make it look like he did it. Go help him! Send the police out here and an ambulance. My dad is hurt. There's no time to waste. Go now."

"Can you breathe in there?" Josh asked.

"Yeah, it's okay," Ricky said. "I see some holes and light. Just hurry and go tell the police. You've got to warn Eddie. His room is down in the basement. Go help him before it's too late."

Josh looked at his friends. They looked back at him with frightened faces.

"I guess we better do as he says," Billy said.

"We're going to go now," Josh yelled "We'll send help."

"Go get Eddie!" Ricky said. "You've got to warn him. Mr. Gossett is the thief. He's the one who set the fires. Tell the police."

"We're going," Josh yelled back. He ran for the paved road. Carlos and Billy were on his heels. The three boys jogged down the side of the road toward Springdale. Josh was breathing hard by the time they reached the place where they had hidden their bikes.

Josh pushed his bike up to the road in a run. He hopped on the seat. He began to pedal. Carlos and Billy were close behind. Josh let them pull up beside him.

"When we get to town, Carlos and I will go warn Eddie," Josh shouted to his friends. "Billy, you get to the nearest phone and call the police. Ask for Deputy Haskins or Sheriff Weaver if they're there. Tell them to send an ambulance out here to Ricky and his dad. And tell them to send someone over to the Bridgewood Apartments. Tell them that Mr. Gossett is dangerous, that he has a gun."

"Okay." Billy nodded his head. The three boys pedaled faster. The long road stretched out before them lonely and empty.

If only a car would come, Josh thought as he looked behind him. But the country road was not well traveled. The boys pedaled faster, driven by the fear and adrenaline they felt in the pits of their stomachs.

They passed woods and fields. In the distance the town of Springdale waited for them. Ricky had said Eddie was in danger, but what kind of danger? Josh didn't understand. But they didn't have time to stop and think about it either. Ricky had been urgent, and there had to be a reason.

Still, so many questions filled Josh's mind as they raced toward town. The bicycles never seemed so slow.

"Oh, no!" Josh looked ahead as they rounded a curve in the road. A long freight train moved slowly as it crossed Drew Road. The engine had just passed by. Josh slowed down.

"Look at all the train cars!" Carlos said. "I can't even see the end of them."

"We can't get across the road!" Billy said.

"This is terrible," Josh said. "What do we do?"

"We could wait it out," Carlos said. Up ahead, the big train clanked and banged. A screeching of metal wheels filled the air as the train came to a stop.

"This could take forever," Josh moaned as he braked his bicycle. "My dad and I sat out here one time for twenty minutes, waiting for a train to move by. He says they have problems sometimes at the grain elevators, or sometimes they have to wait for another train to use the tracks ahead. People in town complain about this intersection, but my dad says that neither the town nor the railroad has enough money to build a bridge for this road."

"Who cares?" Billy asked. "What do we do?"

"I don't know," Josh said.

"We could go over and hit Parker Road," Carlos said. "That's the closest road, and the railroad tracks are on a bridge over it."

"But that will take forever!" Josh fumed.

"We can wait for the train to move," Billy said. "But who knows how long that will take?"

"I can't wait," Josh said anxiously. "Let's go get to Parker Road."

The boys turned their bikes around. They headed away from town. They passed the old blue car in the woods. They reached the intersection and turned on Parker Road.

"Finally," Josh said as they began pedaling down the cement highway. He kept hoping to see another car, but the country road was empty.

By the time they got near town, to the railroad bridge, the train was just moving again, but very slowly. They dipped underneath the bridge and headed into town. They drove on an old gravel road near the railroad tracks as a shortcut back to Drew Road.

The freight train was still blocking the tracks as it rumbled slowly along. Josh looked down the tracks and saw that a long line of freight cars was still to come.

"We did the right thing," Josh panted to his friends, pointing to the remaining cars. Billy and Carlos were too winded to speak. They just nodded. Josh wondered how much time they had lost and if it was too late.

Up ahead, Josh could see the Bridgewood apartment building. They rounded the corner onto Blanchard Road from Drew Road going as fast as they could go.

"Go to the Quick Market up the street and call the police and tell them what you know," Josh called to Billy. The younger boy nodded.

Josh and Carlos pulled into the parking lot of the Bridgewood Apartments. The newly cleaned yard by the playground was filled with old people sitting in chairs and young children playing. A group of boys were shooting baskets at the court.

"Everyone's outside because they are exterminating the building," Carlos said.

"Do you see Eddie?" Josh hopped off his bike.

"No, but I see Mr. Gossett," Carlos said. "Look, he just came out of the recreation room door."

"He's going over to the creek where the bridge used to be," Josh said. "Look, Ricky's mom is over there."

"Yeah, he's saying something to her," Carlos said.

"We've got to find Eddie," Josh said.

"Ricky said he'd be in his room," Carlos replied. "But he wouldn't be in there if they're exterminating, would he?"

"We've got to check," Josh said. "Don't let Mr. Gossett see us."

Josh rode his bicycle to the far side of the big apartment building. He parked on the sidewalk and hopped off. Carlos did the same. The two boys ran to the door at the end of the building that led inside. A handmade sign which said: *STAY OUT! EXTERMINATING!!* was taped to the door. Josh pushed on the handle, but the door seemed stuck.

"I can't get in," Josh said. "The handle turns but something's holding the door back."

"Push harder," Carlos whispered.

"It won't budge," Josh said.

"Let's go around to the front then," Carlos said. "We have to go in and get Eddie."

The two boys ran to the front entrance. A sign warning them to stay out was hung on that door too. Josh quickly tried the front door. But like the side door, it wouldn't budge. From there they could see the playground, and people from the playground could see them.

"People can see us from here," Carlos said.

"I don't know what else to do," Josh replied. "There's another side door."

"But Mr. Gossett might see us," Carlos said.

"We'll just have to risk it." Josh walked quickly around to the side. A sign like those on the other two doors warned them to stay out. "It's stuck too, or locked." Josh looked over by the creek. Mr. Gossett was looking the other way.

"We've got to get in there," Carlos replied. "Where are the police? Do you think Billy sent them here?"

"I hope so." Josh frowned. Then his face lit up. "The recreation room door!"

"But Mr. Gossett would see us for sure," Carlos replied.

"We'll just have to chance it," Josh said.

The two boys walked quickly past the merry-go-round and the slide. Beyond the basketball court was the door that led directly into the old storage room that was now the recreation room. Josh and Carlos walked along the wall.

"Mr. Gossett is facing this way," Carlos whispered.

"I don't care," Josh said. "We've got to get in there."

Josh leaned against the wooden siding on the wall. Only thirty yards away, Mr. Gossett was standing next to Ms. Carson. The big man looked over at Josh and Carlos. He frowned.

"Mr. Gossett, Mr. Gossett!" a voice called. It was Mrs. Perkins, who was sitting under the trees near the new sandbox. The big man glanced at Josh and Carlos suspiciously once more and then walked over to Mrs. Perkins.

"Now!" Josh whispered harshly. Without looking back, he grabbed the handle of the door and turned it. Then he pulled. The door opened. A strong odor filled his nostrils. He and Carlos slipped inside the door. They closed it quickly behind them.

"Those insecticides smell awful." Josh quickly closed the door.

"It smells like a gas station," Carlos replied.

"It does smell like gasoline, doesn't it?" Josh looked around the room. One small window to the outside let light into the room. The Ping-Pong table sat in the middle of the floor. A closet door was open. Balls and bats were hanging on hooks on the closet wall. A cardboard box was sitting on the closet floor.

"That door leads to the hallway," Josh said.

Josh headed for the door that led to the hallway. He turned the knob and the door opened. He stepped into the darkened hallway.

"Whew! That smells terrible," Josh said. "It really smells like gasoline in here."

Josh took a step forward. His foot made a squishy sound.

"The carpet is wet," he said.

Josh bent down. He touched the dark brown carpet with his index finger. He brought the finger back up to his nose and sniffed.

"It is gasoline," Josh said.

"Why would there be gasoline here?" Carlos replied. "Where would it come from?"

Josh shook his head. He looked up and down the hall. He looked behind him.

"It came from that can!" Josh pointed down. In the corner of the hall was a five-gallon gas can. Josh picked it up.

"It's empty," Josh said.

"They don't use gasoline to kill roaches, do they?" Carlos asked.

Josh looked around. Then he looked up at the ceiling. "The fire alarms!" Josh grabbed Carlos by the arm. "Quick, we've got to see if Eddie is in his room."

Josh ran down the hall, turned the corner and ran down the flight of steps in the center of the building. The stairwell was wet with gasoline. The combination of gas fumes and insecticide made his eyes burn. The wet gasoline dripped down the steps to the basement. They followed the trail of gasoline all the way through the boiler room. The big furnace was quiet. The wet trail of gas led all the way into an open door at the other end of the room, which was Eddie's apartment.

The door to his apartment was open. Josh rushed forward. The wet puddle of gas crossed the floor to the bed. He saw Eddie lying on the floor, his legs under the bed. A small wicker trash basket was next to him.

Eddie twitched and groaned. Josh ran over and bent down beside him. He shook his shoulder.

"Eddie!" Josh yelled. "Wake up. Mr. Gossett is trying to set a fire."

"Look, in the corner! Smoke!" Carlos yelled.

Josh turned. In the corner of the room, a curl of smoke drifted up out of the wicker trash basket, which was sitting in a puddle of gasoline. Josh ran over. The smoke came from a cigarette which was wedged inside a pack of matches. The matches sat on top of mounds of white bathroom tissue. Josh grabbed the basket. He ran for the bathroom. He threw it in the shower stall.

Just as it hit the tub, the pack of matches flared up. The tissue paper immediately began to burn. Josh frantically yanked the nearest handle to the shower. The nozzle above him sputtered. The fire in the wicker basket quickly grew bigger. The flames crackled. But after another sputter, cold water rained down from the shower head on top of Josh and the basket. The flames sizzled and hissed as the water poured down. Smoke filled the shower stall. The water poured down in a steady stream. The smoke drifted away. All that was left was a black tarry wad of burnt paper in the bottom of the straw basket.

"It's out," Josh said, running back into the bedroom.

"He's out too," Carlos said. "I can't get him to wake up."

"We've got to get out of here before something else happens," Josh said. "Let's see if we can carry him."

Josh lifted up Eddie's right arm. Carlos grabbed the left. They dragged Eddie across the wet floor. They pulled him out of his apartment into the boiler room. The tile floor wet with gasoline made him easier to drag. When they reached the stairs, Josh put his head under Eddie's arm and then rose up. Carlos did the same. They started up the stairs. Eddie groaned and tossed his head from side to side.

"We'll get you out," Josh said. When they reached the hallway, they headed for the front door. A piece of wood was wedged into the bottom of the door.

"Hold him!" Josh dropped down and pulled the wood with

his fingers. It wouldn't budge. "It's too tight!" Josh yelled.

"The doors are all blocked," Carlos said.

"Let's go out the rec room door." Josh put his head back under Eddie's arm. The boys stumbled down the hallway, dragging Eddie with them. When they got into the rec room, they could hear the sirens.

"Help is coming!" Josh said.

They dragged Eddie across the rec room to the door that led outside. No one was watching as they came outside because all the apartment residents were looking at the two police cars and fire truck pulling into the parking lot.

"I've never been so happy to breathe fresh air," Josh gasped, taking deep breaths. They dragged Eddie over to the slide and laid him gently on the ground. The tall man groaned and coughed, clutching his stomach. He tried to sit up. His eyes opened slightly.

"Josh! Carlos!" Billy yelled from out in the parking lot. He ran over to his friends. He stared at Eddie Reeser lying on the ground. Billy took a step back.

"Is he dead?" Billy asked.

"No, but he's hurt," Josh said. "We've got to get help. Where's Mr. Gossett?"

"He's talking to Deputy Haskins," Billy said. "I told Deputy Haskins everything on the phone. I got here just as they arrived. Mr. Gossett and Ms. Carson were running for Mr. Gossett's car, but Deputy Haskins stopped them."

"Let's go see," Josh said. "We've got to get help for Eddie."

The three boys ran out to the parking lot. Two firefighters were walking toward the front door of the apartment building.

"Carlos, you tell them about the gasoline," Josh said. "A spark could set the whole thing on fire."

"What gasoline?" Billy asked.

"Billy and I will get help for Eddie," Josh continued. "Let's go."

Josh ran toward the fire truck. Billy was at his heels. Mr. Gossett's face was red as he argued with Deputy Haskins across the parking lot. Josh smiled for a moment.

"Quick, you've got to help our friend," Josh yelled out as he reached the fire truck. The men inside the truck jumped out. They carried their big emergency medical cases and followed Josh to the playground.

When they reached the playground area, Eddie Reeser was sitting up, leaning against the back stairs of the slide. He gave Josh a groggy smile. Josh wanted to shout out. Instead, he prayed quietly as the firefighters began to help his friend.

Chapter Eleven

The Bridge Across the Gulf

A week later, the Saturday after Easter, the Springdale Community Church was gathered again at the Bridgewood Apartments. They had just finished a special outdoor worship service under the trees near the playground. People from the Bridgewood and Gateway Apartments had been invited.

The yard was packed with residents of both apartment buildings. The older people were sitting in lawn chairs talking. The little kids were playing on the slide and swing set and the other playground equipment. The young people were playing basketball and throwing Frisbees. Others played Ping-Pong in the rec room. Later on, the people from the church were planning to go across the creek and help the tenants at the Gateway Apartments clean up around their building.

Smoke was curling up from the barbecue grill. Standing in front of the grill, Eddie Reeser was wearing the red-checked apron. His black hair was wet. Ten minutes earlier he had been baptized in the Gateway Apartment swimming pool, along with six other young people. Four of the young people came from the Bridgewood Apartments and two lived in the Gateway Apartments. Eddie hummed as he put hamburger patties on the grill. A man with a long ponytail stood next to Eddie. He was putting plastic bottles of ketchup and mustard on a long table in front of the grill.

Josh, Carlos and Billy stood out by the creek bank watching men erect a new bridge across the creek. Josh walked down into the creek bed and picked up the old metal plate with the blue cross on it. He carried it back up to his friends.

"That's all that's left of the old bridge," Carlos said.

"I'm going to take it home and keep it," Josh said.

"What for?" Billy asked.

"I just like it." Josh looked at the new bridge. It was going to be bigger than the old one.

A young man named Daniel and his sister, Elaine, walked over to join the three boys. Daniel and Elaine lived in the Gateway Apartments. Daniel was ten and on the short side. Elaine was eleven. Both had red hair.

"It was nice of the city parks department to offer to build a new bridge across the creek," Daniel said. "They'll have it finished by today."

"My mom said it was all the publicity in the newspaper that caused the city to build a new bridge," Elaine said. "You guys are heroes for rescuing Eddie and stopping that fire. I don't know how you figured it out."

"Billy helped too," Josh said. "He was the one who noticed

Mr. Gossett changing the batteries. Mr. Gossett put dead batteries in all the smoke detectors. That way the fire would spread before anyone could stop it. He had it planned perfectly. He was going to blame it all on Eddie. He knocked Eddie out with ether. He would have never woken up. They would have found his body in the building afterward. Mr. Gossett would have made it sound like Eddie set the fire and made a mistake somehow and got burned up."

"The police found the stolen video camera and Ms. Carson's necklace in the trunk of Eddie's car," Carlos said. "Mr. Gossett planted them there."

"Yeah, and poor Eddie would have been blamed for the whole thing," Billy said. "Mr. Gossett had already told the police that he suspected Eddie had stolen his camera and Ms. Carson's purse. He also said he thought Eddie might have set fire to the bridge, when he was the one setting all the fires. Mr. Gossett was really clever. He planted just enough suspicion in their minds without actually accusing him."

"Yeah, Deputy Haskins told my dad that Eddie was their prime suspect until they found out what was really going on," Carlos said. "Everyone in the apartment building knew the two of them argued with each other."

Julie, Emily and Rebecca walked over to join their brothers and Daniel and Elaine. They all watched the men putting up the new bridge.

"It's going to be a nice bridge," Daniel said. "Everyone out here will be glad to have it. Are you all going to get in the basketball tournament?"

"Yeah," Josh said. "But I'm not going to play until after we eat."

"Eddie said the food would be ready in about twenty

minutes," Emily said. "Ricky's dad is helping Eddie cook. Did you see him?"

"Yeah." Josh turned to Elaine and Daniel. "He's still got a bandage on his cheek where Mr. Gossett hit him. But he says he feels fine. He's really happy. I really had him figured wrong. When I saw him giving Ricky money for that envelope, I thought it was for drugs or something."

"Ricky said he gave his dad all his homework papers each week," Carlos replied. "His dad gave Ricky child support money, because his mom was spending it all on drugs and alcohol."

"Yesterday the state gave his dad custody of Ricky since his mom is in jail," Josh said.

"She deserves to be in jail," Rebecca said harshly. "She and Mr. Gossett were going to burn down a whole apartment building, kill an innocent man in the process and blame him for the fire. Then they planned to run off together and live happily ever after on the insurance money he collected."

"No one around here knew he was the sole owner of the building," Josh explained. "He always acted like he was just the manager."

"Deputy Haskins said they suspected he might have had some gambling debts or something like that that he needed to pay off," Emily told Daniel and Elaine. "I still can't believe she could cry those big tears and act like somebody stole her money and necklace when she was the one who put her purse in your guitar case. She had everyone fooled."

"Everyone except Ricky and Eddie," Josh said. "It was a clever plan. It might have worked if she hadn't gotten greedy. Ricky said he knew that she didn't have three hundred dollars that could have been stolen around that time of month. That's when he got suspicious. When he asked her about it, she didn't give him a straight answer. That's when he left that first note I found attached to the garbage bag. He wanted to meet with us, but he wanted to investigate it on his own first. Then that night he followed her outside and heard her and Mr. Gossett planning the fire, but he didn't hear all the details. Ricky got scared and ran away. Apparently his mom and Mr. Gossett were both worried that Ricky knew something about their plans."

"Why didn't he just call the police?" Elaine asked.

"Because he didn't hear the whole plan," Josh replied. "And he was afraid and didn't know what to do. He wasn't sure what his mother was up to, but he knew it wasn't good. He was going to ask me, or all of us, to investigate Mr. Gossett and see what we could find out before going to the police. That's why he wanted to meet out far away from town."

"But then Ricky's father got involved," Billy said. "After Chester talked to us that morning, he saw Ricky's dad and told him where Ricky was hiding. Mr. Gossett was already suspicious. Ricky's dad thought he had gotten away unseen, but Mr. Gossett followed him out into the country, hoping he would lead to Ricky. That's when he pulled the gun. Who knows what he would have done with Ricky and his father if we hadn't interrupted his plans?"

"I thought we would never get back to town in time because a train was parked across Drew Road," Billy said to Elaine and Daniel. "We had to go a long ways around to get back here."

"But that delay might have saved us," Josh added. "If we had gotten back sooner, Mr. Gossett would probably have still been in the building with Eddie. If we had walked in on him in the middle of that, who knows what would have happened? He's so big. He probably would have tried to hurt us too. I think God helped us by making us go the long way around."

"You all were so brave," Elaine said to Josh. Josh grinned and looked down at his feet.

"Ricky and his dad said they prayed together in the trunk of the car that whole time until Billy showed the police where they were," Carlos added. "I would have been praying too."

"They were sure both relieved when the police got them out of the trunk of that car," Billy said. "I bet his dad becomes a Christian soon."

Just then, a basketball rolled across the yard to Billy's feet. He picked it up. The words *BRIDGEWOOD REC ROOM* were written in large black letters across the ball.

"Hey, this looks just like your missing ball." Billy examined it. "It's leather and it's the same brand. And look, there's a blue streak of paint. Josh, I think we solved another mystery!"

"It *is* his ball, silly," Emily said.

"But why is Bridgewood's name written on the side?" Billy demanded angrily.

"Because I found it in the rec room closet last Saturday," Josh said. "After the firefighters cleaned up the gas and said it was safe to go back in, I was helping Chester carry stuff outside to air out. I found my ball in a cardboard box in the corner of the closet."

"But how did it get there?" Billy asked suspiciously.

"You know after it was missing and Ricky said he thought he saw Albert Williams pick it up?"

"Yeah," Billy said.

"That's exactly what happened," Josh said. "Albert took

the ball and put it in the box in the rec room closet. He assumed it belonged there. But we all assumed that one of the bridge kids took it, remember? None of us ever checked out Ricky's story and asked Albert. So we weren't very good detectives on that score."

"But why is *Bridgewood* written on the side?" Billy asked as he gave the ball to Josh. "It's not fair that they should keep it! The ball got put in there by mistake!"

"But Josh donated it to their rec room so they would have a good ball," Emily said proudly.

"Really?" Billy said. "You didn't say anything."

"Well, it was supposed to be a secret." Josh looked at Emily carefully.

"I forgot," Emily said. "I'm sorry."

"What's with you two?" Billy asked, looking back and forth between Josh and Emily.

Ricky Carson and Mike Patterson, a boy from the Gateway Apartments, ran over from the court. Josh tossed the ball to Mike. Like Eddie, Ricky's hair was still wet from the baptism.

"Thanks, man," Ricky said. He pointed to the new bridge. "That's going to look really nice. In a way I'm glad that crazy Mr. Gossett set it on fire, because now we'll have a nice new bridge. And everything looks so nice that we're going to keep it and the creek clean."

"Yeah, no one is going to paint on this bridge," Mike said. "We've all agreed and made a pact on both sides of the creek."

"That's right. We want our new bridge to stay nice," Ricky said.

"How's the game going?" Carlos asked.

"It's really great since they added that new backboard at the other end of the court," Ricky said. "Now it's like a real court."

"Only we need bigger teams," Mike said. "You guys want to play?"

"Is it Bridgewood against Gateway?" Emily asked.

"No, it's just teams we picked," Ricky said. "The tournament is after lunch."

"Yeah, this is just a friendly game." Mike tossed the basketball back to Josh. "You want to play or not?"

"I'm in," Josh said with a grin.

"Yeah, me too," Emily said. "And I show no mercy."

"I'll have to pray for you, then," Ricky said with a grin. Josh laughed. He bounced the ball on the ground once, caught it and ran for the court. Soon they all were laughing and joking as they ran up and down the court. The kids not playing cheered from the sidelines.

Billy watched the others running up and down the court. He shook his head back and forth.

"I can't believe Josh would give them his brand-new ball," he said to Carlos. "He loved that ball."

"It's a mystery to me too," Carlos said.

Billy and Carlos looked at each other and shrugged their shoulders. Billy frowned. He looked down at the ground and saw the old metal plate with the blue spray-painted cross. He picked it up.

"Hey, Josh, you forgot your sign," Billy yelled. "Why he would want this old thing is a mystery too. They didn't even spell Jesus' name right. Oh well."

Billy carried the sign over to the court. As they got to the sidelines, Josh scored three points with a long jump shot. Billy and Carlos cheered. Soon they were no longer thinking about mysteries but were lost instead in the excitement of the game.

**Don't miss the next book
in the Home School Detectives
series!**

**Here's a preview of
John Bibee's
*The Mystery in
Lost Canyon***

Chapter Four

The Mountain Trail

"We need to get back on the trail," Kim said flatly. "Are you ready?"

"Just about," Billy said. "Can't we just gallop and catch up?"

"You can't gallop on the trail," Kim said. "It's too rocky and steep and narrow."

"You mean we have to keep walking the horses the whole way to the camp?" Billy asked.

"Of course," Kim said. "It's not a race. That's what a trail ride is. If you want to gallop, you have to wait until we get back to camp. Now let's go."

The four riders headed for the trail. Kim was in the lead. Josh was behind her. Billy followed Josh, and Carlos brought up the rear. They headed up the trail. Occasionally, as the trail twisted and turned up the mountain they could see the glimpses of the other riders.

Josh felt nervous riding right behind Kim. She didn't talk, though she did turn around to check on them to make sure they were keeping up. At a curve on the trail, they passed a patch of lush green grass. Susie stopped and bent her head down to nibble the grass. Kim turned around just at that moment.

"Don't let her eat now," Kim said. "You have to be firm with a horse. Don't let her boss you around."

"I'm trying to be firm," Josh said. "But she pulls down really hard when she wants to eat grass."

At that moment, the big gray horse took a step to grab a tall lazy weed. Josh jerked her head back up. The big horse stamped her foot.

"Don't yank her like that," Kim said. "She has a bit in her mouth."

"You just said to be firm," Josh replied with exasperation. "I'm trying to be firm."

"You can pull her head up firmly without yanking," Kim responded, not trying to hide the irritation in her voice. "Be firm but gentle. How would you like it if someone had a bit in your mouth and yanked hard? You can ruin a horse's mouth by yanking."

Josh just fumed. His face was red from embarrassment. He gripped the reigns of the large gray mare more tightly than ever, determined to keep control of the beast.

"I'd hate to fall off this trail," Billy observed looking down his right. "It really drops away."

"No kidding," Josh said. Looking down the side of the steep mountain made Josh shift in the saddle and held the reigns tighter.

"We're way behind," Kim looked at Josh and frowned. Josh looked up and noticed her staring. "You're holding the reigns too tight," she said.

"I'm trying to steer her on this trail." Josh clenched his teeth. He felt his face getting red again.

"You're riding a horse, not steering a car," the girl reprimanded loudly.

"Well, I don't want her running away or falling off the side of this mountain." Josh's face felt very hot. Anger mixed with embarrassment churned in his stomach. It was bad enough to be corrected in front of his friends Billy and Carlos. But it was worse to be corrected by a girl his own age who was obviously a very good rider.

"We'll catch up with the others eventually," Kim said looking over her shoulder. "There's another stopping place higher up in a meadow near Broken Wing Pass."

They rode toward the sharp turn in the trail. A pile of large boulders made the path very narrow. Josh looked away from the narrow trail for a moment at Kim. She rode on her chestnut stallion, looking as beautiful as only a young cowgirl could look on a bright Colorado morning. As much as he didn't want to admit it, Josh got a knot in his throat looking at her. Kim slowed down right before the curve in the trail, waiting for the others to catch up.

"It's pretty narrow along here, isn't it?" Josh asked nervously.

"Yes," Kim said. "But you can bet your horse wants to stay on the trail even more than you do."

All four riders were as close together as dominoes as they reached the curve. An eerie rattling noise filled the air. Kim's chestnut stallion reared back.

"Rattlesnake!" she yelled, trying to hold onto her horse. The spooked horse cried out in anguish and reared again, backing into Josh and Susie. Susie snorted and whinnied and stamped her feet, trying to stay on the trail as Kim's horse crowded them.

The rattlesnake lunged and so did Flame. The horse cried out and plunged down the steep mountain side. Susie, who was already spooked saw the snake as soon as Kim and Flame left the trail. The snake lunged again and Susie followed Flame. Both horses plunged down the mountainside, their riders struggling to hold on.

Josh yelled as Susie headed down the mountainside. He felt sure the big horse was going to trip and fall and roll over on him any second. Down, down, down the two riders went. Branches snapped and tore at his clothes. More than once he had to duck to keep from being knocked off the horse by a low-lying branch of a spruce or an aspen tree. The ground was a blur beneath his feet.

The horses cried out in sounds of fright as they plunged down the steep mountain. Susie was right on the heels of the chestnut who neighed in anguish as she careened down the steep hill. The trees were thick, but fortunately there was enough room for the horses to dodge them. Instead of slowing down, the horses almost seemed to speed up as if they were gaining momentum like a rolling rock.

"Help us, O God!" Josh cried out as they plunged farther down the mountain. He had never been so scared in all his life. Each jarring step threatened to throw him from the horse's back. They seemed to go forever. There was no stopping since the grade was so steep. The horses stumbled a few times, but kept their feet. The ground and trees became a blur. Josh held his breath, too scared to scream.

Up ahead, the ground flattened for a few yards on the steep mountainside. Flame jerked to the right before he almost ran into an Aspen tree. Kim lost her grip, flew off the horse's back, and hit the ground. Josh and Susie barely missed riding right on top of her. At the last second, Susie turned and followed the runaway Flame. Josh gripped the saddle horn tighter.